CONTI III

CHANGE IS COMING

By Paul Tripi

CONTI III

CHANGE IS COMING

By Paul Tripi

Black Oyster Publishing Company, Inc.

2020

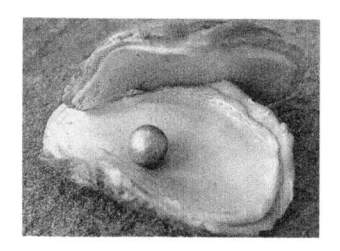

This is a work of fiction. Names, characters, places, and incidents either are the product of the author's imagination or are used fictitiously.
All rights reserved by the author.

CONTI III
CHANGE IS COMING

By Paul Tripi

Chapter 1

Peter Conti sat at a café table in St. Petersburg, Russia drinking a cup of coffee and contemplating the happenings of the past week. The only word that comes to mind to describe the events would be, unbelievable. You see a week ago Peter Conti was one of the heads of the crime syndicate known as the Italian Mafia. Maybe you've heard of it. That's right, a week ago Peter Conti was the GODFATHER.

How that happened is a complicated story so let me start at the beginning.

It all started when Peter was nine years old. How's that for starting at the beginning?

When Peter was nine years old, he met and fell instantly in love with his childhood sweetheart. Her name was Jacqueline Millen. The relationship started out as puppy love but over the years grew into a torrid love affair. It lasted through high school, and college, and got even stronger when Peter was drafted into the Amy and went to Vietnam. Absence makes the heart grow founder. Their relationship was storybook. It was perfect. It is impossible to explain what they were feeling when the Priest had them repeat, "Till death do us part." Peter and Jackie were as much in love as two people could ever be and would have been together forever until those immortal words of the Priest came true. Jackie died. But in Peter's mind they never parted.

That's when his story really started. You see Peter wasn't just another G.I. Joe. He was a remarkable athlete and it showed, especially at boot camp. He was special so the U.S. Army decided to give him more training. When his training was done, he had risen to a unique position. Peter Conti was a Special Forces Green Beret, one of this country's most dangerous killing machines. He became part of a five-man Green Beret stealth unit that played havoc all through Vietnam.

He left the service as the most decorated soldier to come out of the state of New York, holding numerous medals including the Distinguished Service Cross, the second highest medal this county awards. It's second only to the Congressional Medal of Honor. Peter Conti was a dangerous man.

The way his beloved wife died was how Peter ended up in the position of leader of one of the families of the infamous Italian Mafia. His wife was murdered when she was caught in the middle of a Russian Mob hit on a member of the Italian Mafia. She was just an innocent bystander. Peter, who was completely devastated by the loss, turned from a successful peace-loving businessman into a man so full of hate that only revenge could satisfy his torment. He would use his military training and experience and seek out the perpetrators of his wife's death. Peter Conti was going to kill as many members of the Russian Mob as he could. He didn't care if he died trying. He would execute the people responsible until they were all gone, or he was.

In order to accomplish this mission, he called on a man who befriended him as a boy. A powerful man who owned a restaurant that Peter frequented when in college. The man took a liking to the boy and through numerous conversations, became attached to Peter. The man had no children and actually, in his mind, adopted Peter like he was his own. This man's name was Vito Bansano. Unbeknownst to Peter, the restaurant named The Delaware Grill, was just a front for, let's call it, numerous illegal operations. You see Vito Bansano was the Godfather.

There was a war going on between the Italian Mafia and the Russian Mob. The Russians put a contract out on one of the Italians and, during that act; Jackie took a stray bullet and was killed. The Russian's paid in spades. Peter was relentless in his revenge. The media followed the killings and dubbed the killer "The Flower Man" because he left a single long stem white rose on each of his victim's bodies.

Peter had given Jackie a dozen long stem white roses the morning she was killed. You see they were on their way to her obstetrician; Jackie was pregnant with their first child. The roses were meaningful to Peter, but only Peter who lost his wife and his child that morning.

Peter had found out about Vito's alternate position as Godfather years prior, but their friendship was so deep by that time that Peter didn't care. Vito was always good to Peter in every way. Knowing that Vito's operation would be blamed for the Russian deaths, he confronted the man he had grown so close to.

Peter walked into The Delaware Grill with a number of the made men just staring at him. He walked into Vito's office and said, "Vito, I'm sorry for the position I put you in and I figured there are only two things that you can do about it. You can kill me right here and now or you can let me continue my quest."

"Peter, what are you talking about?"

"Vito, I'm the Flower Man."

"Jesus Christ Almighty Peter. What are you saying?"

"When the Russians assassinated your man Gatta, at the bagel shop, my wife was standing close to him. She was killed. I've already killed the ones that pulled the triggers, but until the ones that are truly responsible die, I'm not finished. I am going to kill as many of those sons of bitches as I can. Until they kill me. But I know that my revenge has put you in the middle of it all. For that I am sorry."

"Peter, I have felt the loss of your wife all the way to my core. I share your grief like you are my own son. My men will stay out of this. But if you die know this, they will pay with their miserable lives. I swear it."

Vito walked out of his office and ordered his men to stay away from the Russians. He introduced Peter as the Flower Man and made them swear to secrecy about it but told them to assist Peter with alibis as he continued his pursuit of the Russians.

Peter continued his slaughter. The Russians answered Peter's assault in a big way. Vito Bansano was assassinated.

That triggered Peter in a way that is too difficult to describe. He joined with Vito's men. He more than joined; he near took over. Peter had found a way of killing all the remaining Russians in one fell swoop.

His plan worked out and the remainder of the Russian syndicate was wiped out. The outcome was complete victory for the Italians. This culminated in a windfall of profits for the Italians when they took over all the Russian businesses. Peter was elevated to the position as GODFATHER.

That's how that happened.

It didn't end there. Peter's life was completely changed in many ways of course. His old life with his family and friends had taken a beating. For many reasons he became reclusive, staying away from all the people close to him. He just didn't want them to know what was going on with him behind the scenes. You see Vito Bansano was a very, very rich man and he left almost all his wealth, including The Delaware Grill, to Peter. He also left him his home, which was to put it mildly, a mansion. Peter was filthy rich.

He was rich, but not happy. Jackie was gone.

Peter was a great businessman and converted the organization from head breakers to deal makers. The Mafia became a thriving almost legitimate business. They formed partnerships with their clients and the protection racket turned out to be business ideas that grew the profits for their clients. As Peter put it, "Win,Win."

All was well except for one thing. The Russians. The home office was in Moscow. Igor Terisenko, the head man there, wanted revenge and their businesses back. Twice he sent hit men to take out Peter. That didn't work out too good for them. Peter killed both of the hit men, but not until he found out who sent them.

Peter was living a life he did not choose. Yes, he killed men, a lot of men in his life, a whole lot, but the first of many was during a crazy war. Then, it was for revenge. He had no problem killing the Russian scum that killed his wife. Now the lives he took were for self-preservation. Peter Conti was not a killer at heart. Circumstances put him in the position he's in. He wanted out and had to figure a way for that to happen.

In stepped Jennifer Taylor Grier.

CONTI III

Change is Coming

Chapter 2

Peter followed Vito's wishes to the fullest. One wish was for Peter to go to Vito's hometown in Sorrento, Italy situated on the beautiful Amalfi Coast and along with Vito's brother Gino and family, spread his ashes in the Mediterranean Sea.

Peter was pleasantly surprised at the overwhelmingly warm welcome he received from Gino and his family. It seems that Vito bragged about Peter from the first day they met and continued his praise every time he spoke with his brother Gino. Everything, especially his Army record. After all, Peter Conti was a big-time war hero and Vito bragged about it at every turn. To Vito, Peter was like his adopted son and he made that fact crystal clear to his family. Obviously, Gino and his family were well aware of Vito's feeling towards Peter. Consequently, to them, Peter was family.

Peter was in awe of the beauty of the area, but more importantly reveled in his position in the Bansano family. So much so, he bought a villa there and started calling Gino Bansano, Uncle Gino.

Another wish of Vito's, well it was more than a wish. He expressed in his will that he wanted Peter to continue his charity work. Even though Vito's work was auspicious, his personal life was one of kindness, caring and giving to those in need. Vito had a close relationship with the Mayor of the Buffalo, Robert Stonemetz, and together they did great charity work. The Childrens Hospital was their number one cause. Vito instructed Peter to follow in his footsteps. Peter did just that.

The most negative thing Peter faced when he took over the reins from Vito was that Vito's reputation came with everything. That placed Peter's personal life with his family in peril, especially with his father, Thomas. Everything that Peter inherited from Vito was considered dirty money by his dad. Theresa, Peter's mother, was a typical Italian mom. Her son could do no wrong. Russell, Peter's brother, idolized Peter and would fight ten men with only a wooden spoon as a weapon to defend him. He loved his brother. Marie, Peter's baby sister, just loved Peter no matter what, period. Peter's in-laws, the Millens loved Peter as well, but Peter stayed away from them after Jackie's death. He just couldn't face them. It hurt too much.

Peter needed to change or at least shrink that reputation and he thought he could do that if he nestled up to the Mayor and joined him in his quest to make the Buffalo Children's Hospital one of the finest in the country. They met and an uncanny bond was formed between them. Peter dove headfirst into the cause. Maybe, because along with the death of his wife he lost his unborn child, and for that reason helping sick and needy children struck home even more. Mayor Stonemetz did his part to help change Peter's negative reputation into a strong positive one by utilizing the media to broadcast Peter's fame as a war hero. It all worked. Peter was now looked upon by a grateful city as a prominent generous businessman. He was welcomed on the board of directors of The Childrens Hospital by the all the other members on the board and his friendship with the Mayor grew with every meeting. The whipped crèam on top of all this is when Mayor Stonemetz threw a fundraising shindig at his home to introduce Peter to the other members of the board and a number of big-time contributors. This party was really all about the hopes that they would reach into their pockets and purses and give. Peter's family and in-laws were invited. It changed how they looked at Peter. Using Peter's words win, win.

He later took them to his new home, or more accurately stated, his mansion, and the looks on their faces spoke a thousand words. The transition was complete. Except for one indisputable fact, Peter Conti was still THE GODFATHER.

This is where his story really gets interesting.

Peter was trying to legitimize the Organization. The Mafia is not a bunch of guys who go around willy nilly and just kill people for fun. It is a business and Peter was trying to run it as such. It was working and working well. The members of the crew were earning money like they never had before and there was little to no arm breaking at all. Peter operated the crew like a business and even incorporated the operation and called it the Zorde Acquisition Group. He did that so all their incomes would be taxable but legitimate. It all made sense, people go to jail for tax evasion. This protected everyone.

Business was running like a well-oiled machine and other than the two times the big boss from Russia sent a couple of mobsters to kill Peter, everything was good. Of course, that's not a small thing and Peter wanted that to stop. But how? Peter needed to figure out a way.

Tony Sotto was Vito's right hand man and heir to Vito's title and position. Tony was a wise and loyal man to the operation, and it was he who elevated Peter over himself to the position of Godfather. He of course became Peter's right hand man and did his job well.

Peter knew that the Russians were trying to bust their way back into the region. It was obvious because they had already sent men to investigate what the Italians were doing and of course, kill Peter while they were there. They did that twice. Their bodies were never found. Peter knew a war was brewing. He also knew many of their men would die if that happened. He decided to strike a deal with Tony Sotto, a deal that would put Tony in his rightful position as the Godfather and Peter could get out. It was simple; Peter would resurrect The Flower Man, go to Russia, and eliminate Terisenko and as many other of the top Russians heads as needed. This would leave them the message that lets them know that, if they wanted a war, the Mafia can easily come to Russia. The dead bodies of the bosses will be proof enough that the Italians mean business. Simply stated, the Russians need to keep their business in Russia and Peter's organization will keep their business in the States. Peter laid all that out to Tony. He explained that what he had accomplished what he originally set out to do; revenge his wife and Vito's deaths and semi-legitimize the operation into an even more profitable situation for all the men. With this plan the war with the Russians would be over, Tony would get his rightful position as the Godfather, and Peter would be out. He also realized that he knew a great deal, maybe too much, about the operation, which was not a good thing, but he made it clear that he was aware that they knew enough about him to put him away forever. Tony's response was simple, since all the men were thrilled with the increase in revenue, they were enjoying due to Peter's direction, he foresaw no objection. The deal would be consummated when Peter eliminated the Russian competition. When that was done, Tony guaranteed that everyone would be sworn to secrecy. The deal was struck.

Now how does Peter get to Russia without scrutiny? That's where Jennifer Taylor Grier comes into the picture.

Mayor Stonemetz called Peter and asked if he would have lunch with him and a guest from Washinton D.C., a woman who wanted to get involved in The Childrens Hospital charity. Her name was Jennifer Taylor Grier. Peter jumped at the chance to meet her.

Why?

Jennifer Grier is the United States Ambassador to the Soviet Union.

CONTI III

Change is Coming

Chapter 3

That brings us back to Peter sitting at the Café in St. Petersburg, Russia.

FLASHBACK
(In Italic's)

Jennifer Taylor Grier.

Jennifer Taylor Grier.

What a Godsend for Peter and just at the perfect time. The Russian syndicate was knocking at his door and Peter's plan was to take the fight to them. What luck. If he could somehow sweet-talk this Jennifer woman into a date, after all she is a single woman and the Mayor said pretty, he could utilize the connection. Maybe just maybe, he could start a relationship, one that would be instrumental for his needs. Question is, is she even available? He had to try. This was too perfect to pass up. She must spend a goodly amount of time in Russia. What better alibi could he have then to go there because he was visiting a lady friend? He hadn't dated any woman other than Jackie since he was 16 years old, but he was quite a handsome and successful man. He did have that going for him. It was worth a try. He really didn't know what to do and he knew it, but he had to try.

"This is stupid," he thought to himself. "But what do I have to lose?"

He had almost talked himself out of it until she exited the car. Peter's heart was pounding. He did not expect her to look like she looked. She was breathtakingly beautiful. Peter was speechless for a moment, but was able to eke out, "Excuse me for staring Miss Ambassador. Bob said you were a lovely woman, but he didn't say you were stunning. It is such a great pleasure to meet you. Peter Conti at your service."

"How do you do Mr. Conti? My name is Jennifer Taylor Grier. The pleasure is mine. Bob hasn't stopped talking about you since we got in the car. Your resume is impressive Sir."

"Bob exaggerates. Yes I did save all 50 of those babies from that burning building, but anybody would have repeatedly jumped back into the roaring flames to do that. Is that what you told her Bob?"

"No Peter. I told her you were in the Army."

"Well that too."

All three laughed.

They walked in and Peter got his usual greeting from the owner.

"Mr. Mayor, a pleasure to see you again Sir and hello Peter. Every time you come in you surprise me. This time you come in with the Mayor and I'm assuming Miss America."

Peter laughed out loud, "Antonio Scavazzo this is the U.S. Ambassador to the Soviet Union, Miss Jennifer Taylor Grier."

Antonio snapped his fingers and Pasquale Tocco, Antonio's headwaiter, escorted the small group to Peter's private table.

"What can I get your party to drink Mr. Conti?"

"Son of a bitch. I'm the Mayor and he asks you?"

"What can I say Bob. It's all about those 50 babies."

They all laughed again.

With a smile that would knock a buzzard off of a dead cow, the Ambassador said, "Have you ever been here before, Mr. Conti?"

"As a matter of fact, I have. Miss Grier. And is there any chance you could call me Peter?"

"I would be happy to. If you call me Jennifer."

"Wait, what am I a piece of bologna over here?"

"Excuse me Bob, but have you noticed how pretty this woman is? I'm just saying."

"Shut up. I want to talk business," injected the Mayor.

"What business?"

"Jennifer here is originally from our sister city, Rochester, and is very interested in helping with our Childrens Hospital Charity Drive."

"That's right Peter. I was involved before when I was a congresswoman living in Rochester. It's a marvelous cause and I would like to help in any way I can."

"How long will you be in town, may I ask?" asked Peter.

"I'll be here through the weekend. A very close friend of mine is getting married Saturday. I'm not leaving until late on Sunday."

"Great. That will give me a few days to put something together."

The lunch went perfectly. Just before they were getting ready to leave, Antonio's daughter came over to the table, kissed Peter on the cheek and, as usual, told him how grateful she was.

As she walked away, the Mayor said, "I never asked you what that was about?"

"Great kid isn't she. I helped her out of a jam awhile back and she has never forgotten. It was my pleasure, believe me."

He left it at that and said, "Jennifer, not to be bold, but I'm having a small dinner party at my home this evening. That would be a perfect time for us to discuss some possibilities. If you don't have plans, I would love to have you attend."

"As a matter of fact, I have no plans for the evening. That sounds lovely. I would love to."

"Who's attending?" she asked.

"Just you and me," he said with a smile.

"You are something else Mr. Conti. Are you serious?"

"Actually, I am. It would be a good time to discuss some strategies, but if you think I'm being forward."

"No, you're right. I accept."

"Bob, would you and Arlene like to join us?" asked Peter.

"I'd love to Peter, but unfortunately we have a previous engagement."

"Sorry you can't make it, my friend," answered Peter.

Peter turned to Jennifer and asked, "Where are you staying Jennifer?"

"I'm at the Ritz."

"Then I'll send a driver to pick you up. Is 7:30 Okay with you?"

"You were right Bob. This guy is something else. 7:30 would be perfect Peter."

Peter called for the check. Antonio came over and said, "Peter, how many times do I have to tell you, there is no check for you my friend. You are always my guest."

"Antonio, I hate that. But thank you."

The two men shook hands and Antonio said his polite goodbyes to Peter's guests. Peter threw two hundred-dollar bills on the table for a tip and they got up to leave.

"Thank you, Peter. You are such an easy touch. You know that?" said the Mayor.

"Bob, anytime my friend. Anytime. Miss Jennifer Taylor Grier I look forward to seeing you again this evening. Enjoy the rest of your day."

"Thank you, Mr. Peter Conti. I look forward to it Sir."

Peter drove straight home to let Hazel, his housekeeper and cook, know he was having a guest for dinner. The entire time he was driving he thought about how he could use the Ambassador for entry into Russia. It was perfect. There was only one problem. He really liked her. She was perfect. He felt terrible using her, but it was too perfect to let slip through his hands. He knew he had to keep his feelings out of it. But it was going to be difficult. Plus, he never did question her to see if she was involved with anyone. She could be living with someone for all he knew. He needed a plan. Access to Russia would be instrumental to his cause.

Jennifer arrived at the front door at 7:45. She looked like a movie star. Peter greeted her on the stairs leading to the giant entry doors. Her beauty was memorizing. Peter walked her through the doors into the foyer.

He gave the nickel tour, not the full nine yards. He didn't want to seem like he was showing off. They ended up on the patio outside of the kitchen area just off the pool. The area consisted of an array of lounging pool seating and a number of patio tables and chairs. One of the tables was set up with service for two. Peter served wine, but had the makings for a vodka martini on hand. She chose the wine.

"Do you live here alone Peter?" she asked.

"No. Hazel lives here with me."

"Oh, Bob told me you were a widower."

Just then Hazel came out carrying a tray with a variety of hors d'oeuvres.

"Would you care for any hors d'oeuvres Miss?"

"Just put them down on the table Hazel. We'll snack on them a little later. She is plying me with wine right now. She's so obvious."

Hazel just laughed. He always made her laugh.

"Yes Sir," she said still giggling.

"That's Hazel?" she asked.

"Yeah. Isn't she great?"

"You know she calls me Peter when no one's around. Couldn't live here without her."

"Peter, I was kind of referring to a companion when I asked if you lived here alone."

"Oh, no, I live here alone," he said with a sly smile. "I'm unattached. How about you?"

"My position keeps me too busy for that, although I get hit on every day. It's maddening sometimes."

"Me too," he said almost laughing.

"I bet you do. You're not that disgusting looking."

Just what Peter wanted to hear, joking and familiarity.

"Disgusting looking? Now I can see I wasted my time washing under my arms with a washcloth just cause I knew you were coming."

Jennifer burst out laughing.

Just then Hazel came out, "We have Cornish game hen or steak or both miss. Which do you prefer?"

"The game hen sounds lovely. Thank you Hazel."

"You're welcome Miss. And you Sir?"

"The bird sounds nice. Thanks Hazel. Oh Hazel, how long before you plan on serving?"

"Up to you Sir. Would an hour suit you?"

"Perfect. One more thing Hazel, would you please bring out another bottle of wine?"

The dinner was perfect. The conversation was light, but interesting. Jennifer talked about her duties in Russia without giving away any trade secrets. Peter just said he had his fingers in a number of businesses and that business was good. After dinner they were having an aperitif, in this case a glass of Sherry, and then some coffee. Then out of the blue Jennifer asked, "Peter, would I be too invasive if I asked you about your time in Vietnam. I'm sorry, but Bob was saying some braggadocios things about you. If I struck a bad cord, please don't answer."

"Gee Jenny, I mean Jennifer."

"Oh please, Jenny is fine."

"Well, I bet he didn't tell you I was scared the entire time I was there."

"No, he told me you were the most decorated soldier to come out of this state when you were over there. He told me you were Special Forces Green Beret."

"Oh yeah. That too, I forgot. Yes I was that."

She laughed, "Peter, come on, tell me something, I'm interested."

"Jenny. Did you ever hear the expression WAR IS HELL? Well, whoever said that was right. You have guys dying all around you and all you can think of is what can I do to stop this. That's what I tried to do. Yes, no denying, I definitely took lives. It's so terrible to even say that, it still haunts me. BUT I was teamed up with four other Green Beret soldiers and we made a pretty impressive unit. All I can say is that we saved countless American lives. That's what I'm proud of, not the medals. I hope that's enough information about that for you."

"It is Peter, thank you."

"We didn't get a chance to talk much about the Hospital Charity Drive. I have been kicking around a few ideas, but it's late. Any chance you have some time tomorrow? I know you must have a busy schedule, but if we could meet maybe for lunch," asked Peter.

"I'm on vacation. I have no schedule. This has been an absolutely wonderful evening and you are a charming man. I would love to see you again tomorrow."

"Does that mean, Yes?"

Then something happened that staggered Peter for a second, bringing back memories of the love of his life. After he said that, Jennifer slapped him on the shoulder, exactly the way and exactly in the same spot as Jackie. He hesitated before saying anything and, as he found his way back to reality, he said, "Owww. Oh my God you broke my arm."

She hit him again. Same spot. Just like Jackie.

Of course Peter felt nothing. Peter is not only extremely handsome; he's also built like a brick shithouse.

"So that does mean yes," he replied.

"Yes. Is that more clear?"

"Great. How about having lunch over in Canada at Niagara Falls?"

"Are you hitting on me Mr. Conti?"

"Noooo. Well, maybe a little. Are you offended?"

"Not in the least. I was just about to hit on you."

This time Peter burst out laughing.

"Come on. I'll take you back to your hotel. What do you think about starting our lunch outing about 9:00 AM?"

"That's a little early for lunch don't you think."

"Well, I was thinking about starting lunch out with a little breakfast. What do you say? Do you have the time?"

"I say, you move very fast Mr. Conti."

"Well?"

"Sounds great."

"I'll ring you up just at 9:00. Try and look a little better than you did tonight."

"Sir. I resent that comment," she said laughing.

"Well maybe you didn't understand what I was saying. What I meant by that is, you can try and look better tomorrow than you do tonight, but I am very aware that that would be nearly impossible because you look absolutely stunning tonight."

"Now there's a line for you."

"Did it work?"

"Maybe."

"Let me take you back before I do something I'll regret."

"What do you mean by that Sir."

"This."

Peter didn't want to take this chance, but it seemed like a good idea at the time. He reached over and kissed her. Not a passionate kiss, but definitely a kiss.

"Well, that was unexpected," she said.

"I'm sorry. I couldn't help myself," he said.

"I would have been mad if you didn't."

He took her back to the Ritz and left.

Peter showed up the next morning right on time and buzzed her room. Five minutes later Jennifer walked out of the elevator casually dressed.

"Well I'll be," said Peter.

"What do you mean by that?"

"I really thought that it would be impossible for you to look prettier than you did last night. But I was wrong. You look radiant."

"Are you starting with lines at 9:00 o'clock in the morning?"

"That's not a line. You look great."

"You must be a fantastic salesman is all I can say."

"Jenny, fact is fact."

"Well then, thank you. You don't look so bad yourself."

"Thanks, I took a shower, too."

She laughed and said, "Would you like to have breakfast right here in the dining room?"

"No. I have a place in mind that I really think you'll like. The atmosphere is very pleasant and the food is great."

"OK, sounds very nice, let's go."

They headed over to Allen Street, a quaint area in Buffalo that somewhat emulates Greenwich Village in New York, for a light breakfast at one of its open cafes.

They pulled up to Yaya's Bistro and Bakery, were seated at a comfortable table with a very nice view, and ordered coffee to start.

Peter was even more torn as he gazed across the table at Jenny. The sun was framing her outline and her face was like an angel's. It didn't matter. He needed this connection. He somehow had to stay focused on the task at hand. But it was getting harder and harder by the minute.

"I love this place Peter. Thank you."

"You are welcome. I knew this would suit you."

"How do you know that? You barely know me."

"Please. You may be complicated when it comes to government work, but I saw the real you last night; warm, caring, funny, and smart, but down to earth. Best way I can explain it is, I see a woman who is complex when she needs to be, but simple when it comes to life. Plus, you're here because a good friend, a friend who is almost like family, is getting married. U.S. Ambassadors don't do that kind of thing unless they are big time family and friend oriented. Look, I know you are beautiful on the outside, anybody can see that, but what I learned last night about you is that you're even more beautiful on the inside. There, you happy now, you made me embarrass the shit out of myself in less than a half an hour."

"I'm the one who's embarrassed. Wow. You really must be horney!"

"I didn't say that because of that. I said that so that you might pick up the check!"

Jenny laughed so hard she almost spilled her coffee.

The rest of the breakfast was spent laughing and joking and just having a great time. Peter was sweeping her off her feet. This was not working out the way he wanted. You see, Peter was falling for her as well. He needed another plan.

Business. There had to be a way he could combine business with pleasure. But he couldn't think of anything, anything at all. His brain was on hold. All he could do was stare at Jenny. Is it possible he thought to himself? Is it possible to fall in love again? He wasn't sure, but it sure felt like it because everything he'd said and done at least to this point had nothing to do with business and everything to do with the woman he was with. She was wonderful in every way.

They hopped back into Peter's two-seater Mercedes and started towards Niagara Falls. Peter decided he could kill two birds with one stone by taking a two-mile detour.

"Jenny, would it be an inconvenience, well not really an inconvenience, more like a horrible chore, if we made a quick stop."

"Now what? I'm not sure I trust you."

"It's my parents. They have been all over me for a long time to date again. I'm too busy for that, but since this is sort of a date, would you mind just saying hello? Just a minute or two, really, it will definitely get them off my back.

"That's not a chore. That would be a pleasure. I would love to meet them."

"Yeah, you say that now."

"No. Really."

"Great, you have no idea how much an Italian mother can nag."

She laughed.

A few minutes later they were parked in his parent's driveway.

"You're sure now."

"Peter, no problem."

"Okay. I warned you."

Peter sauntered into the kitchen just ahead of Jenny. His mother and father, along with his brother Russell and sister-in-law Colleen, were sitting at the table having coffee.

"Jesus Christ. Look what the cat dragged in," said Russell.

"Hi everyone. Just dropped in for a minute. We're on our way to the Falls. Everyone, this is Jennifer Grier."

"Hiii," she said.

"Jenny, this is my mom Theresa and dad Thomas. This beautiful woman is my sister-in law and she had the misfortune of marrying my brother Russ."

"It is a pleasure meeting all of you."

Russ spoke first. "Sorry that you're blind Jennifer, but really he's not that terrible a looking guy."

"I think he's handsome."

"Please come in. Sit down. Let me fix you something to eat," said Theresa.

"Oh thank you, but no. We just had breakfast," she answered.

"How about some coffee?" asked Thomas.

Peter answered, "We just stopped in to say hello. We're going to run."

"NO WAY," said Theresa. "We want to meet your lady friend."

"Let's stay for a cup of coffee Peter," injected Jenny.

"You asked for it."

"My God you're pretty," said Colleen.

"Takes one to know one," Jenny responded.

"I like her Peter," said Colleen.

"Are you a model?" asked Thomas.

"DAD!"

"No Mr. Conti, I am the United States Ambassador to the Soviet Union."

The entire group's mouths dropped open and there was a moment of complete silence.

"It's just a job," she said.

"Jesus Mary and Joseph, Peter," said Russell. "How in the world did you talk this beautiful, intelligent, successful woman into even getting in a car with you."

"I used my charm and good looks AND I bought her breakfast."

"Jennifer, not only are you all the things my son Russ just said, you're also brave," said Thomas.

"He's not that bad after you get to know him."

"That's all. I'm not punishing this woman with you people anymore. I'm taking her to the Falls."

"Come back for dinner," pleaded Theresa.

"I'd love to Mrs. Conti but I have a previous engagement. Maybe next time."

"Not one person said a word to me. Nothing. I feel slighted," said Peter.

"Okay, here are some words, go take this lovely woman to the Falls and call your mother more often. She's always saying, why doesn't he call?"

"I'm sorry. You know I love you mom."

"AWE, I love you too Peter."

"She never ever says that to me! Never," said Russell.

"You want some cheese with that whine," answered Peter.

Everybody laughed.

"We're going."

"It was so nice meeting you all," expressed Jenny.

"The pleasure was ours sweetheart," answered Theresa. "Come back anytime."

Peter got in the car and quickly said, "Now I owe you big time. Your wish is my command."

"Okay. I just thought of something."

"Name it."

"How would you like to go to a wedding tomorrow?"

"NO, absolutely NOT. Wait, do you mean with you? Then, yes of course."

"Great, you just became my plus one."

They had a fantastic time at the Falls, in fact, the entire rest of the day. It was getting late in the afternoon when Jenny said, "Peter, I don't want this day to end, but I really do have a previous engagement. It's with a bunch of my girlfriends from the wedding party that I haven't seen for ages. I need to get back to the hotel to get ready."

"Of course. I understand completely. I guess you can call me with the times and the whatnots for tomorrow. If you still want to go with me. I'm just giving you a chance to let yourself off the hook."

"Don't be silly. I can't wait until tomorrow. I think I'm starting to like you Peter Conti. A lot. Let me get to the room and make some calls. I'll call you within the hour and let you know my schedule for tonight and tomorrow."

"Sounds great."

They were on their way back to the Ritz. When they were getting close, a couple of blocks away, Jenny asked Peter to pull over. This time she kissed him and wow what a kiss.

Peter was caught, hook, line, and sinker.

*   *   *

"Gwen, it's Jenny."

"Where have you been girl? We all thought we'd see you today."

"Busy. I just called to see what time the girls are getting together tonight and I need times and places for tomorrow."

"Don't give me that busy answer. What's up?"

"Gwen. I met someone?"

"Shut your mouth. Tell me everything."

"He's so handsome he makes me melt. He's successful, built like a pro football player, and smart. He's funny and makes me laugh, all the time."

"Stop it, you're going to make me call off my wedding. All of a sudden Joe's not sounding that great."

"Shut up. Joe's perfect for you."

"I know. Who is he? How did you meet?"

"He's on the Board of Directors of the Childrens Hospital and we met at lunch yesterday. Mayor Stonemetz introduced us. We had lunch at a beautiful Italian restaurant. Maybe you've eaten there, Antonio's."

"Yes, on special occasions. The place is always so packed it's near impossible to get reservations."

"Peter has a private table there and they treated him like he was a king. The owner spent time with us and told him to stop asking for checks because Peter will always be his guest. Peter dropped a few hundred on the table anyway, but my jaw dropped when Antonio said that. Then Antonio's daughter came over and kissed Peter on the cheek and thanked him for I don't know what, but thanked him just the same. It was unreal."

"Peter who? Who is this guy?"

"A friend of the Mayors, his name is Peter Conti."

"Peter Conti, I know that name. The war hero guy they've been writing about in the papers?"

"Yes, but he doesn't talk about that. Gwen, he's the one! I'm bringing him to the wedding."

"Holy shit, and you just met him yesterday?"

"Yes, but after lunch he asked if I was available to attend a dinner party he was throwing at his home to discuss a charity thing for the Childrens Hospital. I said that I was free and asked who would be there. He said, just you and me. I had to laugh, but I went. Oh my God, you should see his house and it was a perfect night."

"Did you?"

"Stop it, we just met. BUT I wanted to. Does that tell you anything?"

"You'll meet him tomorrow. Tonight is for us girls."

"Change of plans. The guys are coming too. About a half dozen couples, Joe and I, Joe's brother Steve and his wife the other Jenny, Judy and Dan, Frankie Ann and Al, Georgette and Kurt, Karen and

33

Rafael, Joe's and you guys if you're not embarrassed of us peon's, Miss Ambassador."

"Where and what time?"

"We're meeting at The Cabaret on Main Street at 8:00."

"Great. I'll be there. I have no idea if Peter is available, but I'll ask."

"I would love to meet him. I am so happy for you Jenny. It's about time."

"SHUT UP. Can't wait to see you."

"Me too. See you later."

Jenny hung up the phone and hesitated for a few minutes but decided she only had a few more days before she had to head back to Russia, so what the heck.

"Peter, it's Jenny."

"Who?"

"Jenny Grier, oh stop it."

"Do you know your schedule?" he asked.

"That's why I'm calling. Tonight my girlfriends and I were getting together, but the plan changed and they're bringing their husbands. I was wondering if you had plans for the evening and, if you didn't, maybe you might want to join me?"

"Sorry Jenny, I'm cleaning my bowling ball tonight."

Jenny laughed out loud right over the phone.

"Great," said Peter. "I'd love to. Where, when, and what do you want me to do?"

"Just pick me up at the hotel around 7:45. Do you know The Cabaret on Main Street? A number of my friends are meeting there at 8:00. This way you'll have a chance to meet Gwen and Joe, the bride and groom, and a bunch of my childhood friends."

"That sounds wonderful AND I get to spend more time with you."

"You're still horney aren't you?" she said giggling."

"No comment," he responded immediately. "I'll buzz your room."

"You always make me laugh. See you soon."

Peter drove up to the front door of the nightclub called The Cabaret in his beautiful Mercedes to drop Jenny off before he parked. Gwen, Joe, Georgette, and Kurt were standing there talking when he pulled up. Jenny got out and immediately hugged them all while Peter parked. The group waited for Peter.

"Everybody, this is my date, Peter Conti. Peter this is the bride to be Gwen who I've known since I was a girl. In fact, I've known all these people all my life it seems. This is Joe her almost husband and this is Georgette and her husband Kurt."

"A pleasure meeting you. Thank you Gwen and Joe for inviting me," said Peter politely.

"Is that a joke," said Gwen. "When Jenny told us she met someone, we couldn't wait to meet you. You're right Jenny he IS handsome."

Jenny responded with, "He's taken and you're getting married tomorrow."

"Oh Yeah, I forgot for a second. Joe, you're even more handsome honey so don't get jealous."

"Jealous, what are you talking about? I think he's handsome too!"

Everybody laughed and went inside. Peter met the rest of the crew that were already seated and the night began. It was a terrific night for everyone. Drinking, dancing, laughing, everyone there was having a great time and then the trouble started. A few of the guys who were standing at the bar were staring at Jenny all night. Peter noticed but said and did nothing. He was watching though. Finally Jenny and Gwen got up to go to the ladies room and two of the guys walked over to them. They said something rude to the woman and Jenny retorted quite loudly. One of the guys reached for her arm. Peter was there like a cat. He wasn't polite or politically correct at all when he said, "What the fuck do you think you're doing?"

"This ain't none of your business buddy."

"I'm making it my business," said Peter as the other two guys rose from their bar stools.

Peter turned and calmly said to Jenny's friends, "Sit down guys, I got this."

"Who the hell do you think you are?" asked the guy who had reached for Jenny's arm.

"Somebody you really don't want to mess with. So, if I were you, I would apologize to these ladies, pay your bar tab, and leave quietly or you will be leaving in an ambulance."

Joe, Steve, Kurt, Dan, and Rafael weren't about to sit this out even though their wives were trying to keep them out of it.

Joe said to Peter, "Conti. We're right behind you."

"Conti? Did you say Conti? Peter Conti?" said the loud mouth as all four of the hoods took a few steps back. The leader continued with, "I'm sorry Mr. Conti. We didn't mean anything by this. Nothing at all I swear. We we're just fooling around. We'll be leaving now. Have a nice evening."

They paid their bill and were gone just like that. Joe turned to Peter and asked what everyone in their party wanted to know, "Peter, who the hell are you?"

"I guess they thought I was that Green Beret guy they've been writing about in the paper," answered Peter.

"Jesus," said Joe.

Peter addressed the table and said, "Hey everybody it's over. Don't let this little disturbance spoil the night."

Gwen turned to Joe and whispered, "Jenny told me Peter IS that guy from the paper."

They had no idea that it wasn't the Green Beret thing that had those hoodlums shitting their pants. They had no idea at all.

Everyone returned to their seats at the table, everyone but Peter and Jenny that is.

"Are you OK honey?" said Peter realizing it was the first time he called her that.

"Just fine Peter. Tarzan to the rescue."

"Don't be silly. Bullies always back down. But excuse me, I have to change my underwear. I think I soiled myself."

Jenny laughed again. She laughed hard, but this time it was Jennifer Taylor Grier, the United States Ambassador who was caught, hook, line, and sinker.

Jenny was definitely smitten; no, that's an understatement, she was falling in love. She held onto Peter's arm tight with both hands as they walked to the car. She was already dreading the fact that she was leaving and going back to Washington, D.C. on Sunday, from there on

37

to Russia. She didn't want to leave. Peter drove her back to her hotel. She gave him a passionate kiss in the car and said,

"Stay with me tonight Peter."

Peter hesitated a moment. He shook his head as to say, I don't know what to do, and said, "I want to more than anything in this world Jenny, but I can't."

"Why?"

"There are things that are said about me that could hinder your position as an Ambassador and I don't want you to take that chance."

"What things? I don't understand."

"When Bob told you about me, did he explain how I obtained a big portion of my wealth?"

"No. Not really. He just said you were a hell of a businessman."

"He's right about that, I am. I do well. But my house and a number of my investments came from a very wealthy man. A man who semi-adopted me and, when he died, left me many things."

"I don't care about that Peter. I just want to be with you."

"Yes I understand Jenny, I want to be with you too. But let me finish."

"I don't understand what this has to do with anything."

"This man's name was Vito Bansano. Jenny, he left me more than just his house, his reputation went with it as well."

"What are you talking about? What do you mean reputation?"

"His reputation is why it's so important we have this conversation. It was rumored that he had his fingers in racketeering. That he was a gangster. I'm Peter Conti not Vito Bansano. The thing that stinks *about it all is Vito was a good man. That being said, I'm worried that any affiliation with me could be bad for you. That would break my heart. That's why I won't go up with you. Someone might recognize me. As much as it is something I want to do more than anything else in the world, I can't let you take that chance. Do you understand?"*

"Yes. Peter I understand. I can't believe I'm saying this, but you leave me no choice. There is only one thing that I can do."

"Don't say it. You are going to break my heart if you do."

"Let's go to your place. I don't need to go into the hotel. I'm sure you have something I can sleep in."

Peter just smiled and said, "I think I can find something."

They woke up early. Well to be honest they barely slept. They got cleaned up and went down for coffee. Peter's mind was in a quandary. His grand scheme to use this woman for entry into Russia and as an alibi was completely kaput. There was no way no how he would or could follow up on that line of thinking and for good reason. He was head over heals in love with her. But how could this work between them. She's a United States Ambassador and he's a, well he doesn't know what the hell he is anymore. Last night changed him. He needed another plan.

He stared across the table at her without saying a word. She was doing the same. Both of their minds were spinning. Hers because she was leaving the next day and the thought of leaving him was killing her and his because he's still The Godfather of a crime family, for Christ sakes. What a dilemma.

She broke the silence, "Peter, I want to say something."

"Jenny, we've only known each other a few days."

"How do you know what I'm going to say?"

"Because I want to say the same thing and I can't believe it. I don't know what to do."

"What are we going to do? I don't want to leave," said Jenny. Then followed with," I love you Peter."

"There, you went and said it."

"Don't you dare."

He stopped her in mid sentence by putting his fingers to her lips and said, "I love you too. We will work this out. Jenny, you know I'm a widower. That's all you know. What you may not know is that I loved my wife with every fiber of my being. I never thought in a million years I could ever feel that way again. But then I met you. We will work this out. But not today, today we are going to a wedding."

"You are a smart man Peter Conti."

"That's because I have a giant QI."

Jenny just laughed.

"Sweetheart the wedding doesn't start until 5:00, what do you want to do until then?" He hesitated for a second and with a giant smile said, "Besides that."

"You decide. I just want to be with you."

"Well, my mother did say come back soon and I would like you to meet my parents under different circumstance then yesterday's. Let me put it this way, our relationship has changed since then. I could invite them over for breakfast."

"That would be very nice. But why don't we go there? I'll bet they would be much more comfortable."

"I'll call."

The entire family was there and thrilled that Peter was bringing a woman over for the second day in a row. They all knew what that meant and, to be honest, they thought that would never happen again.

When they walked in Jenny spoke first. "Hi everyone. I hope we're not imposing?" *said a smiling Jenny.* "And hello to you, you must be Marie. What a pleasure to meet you."

"Yes I am and hello Jennifer Taylor Grier, United States Ambassador to the Soviet Union."

"Its just Jenny."

"Hi Jenny, the pleasure is all mine. Everyone said you were pretty, but they were wrong, you're gorgeous."

"That's enough sis, I already got the job," *joked Peter.*

"Sit down honey, coffee?" *asked Peter's mom.*

"Thank you, Mrs. Conti, that sounds wonderful," *answered Jenny.*

They had a lovely breakfast. Everyone was interested and asked Jenny a bunch of questions about her position and about Russia and what not and Jenny reciprocated by asking them questions about their jobs and stuff. You know normal chitchat. They also asked her how long she would be in town. It was pleasant.

"Unfortunately, I'm leaving tomorrow for Washington, D.C. and then on to Moscow."

"Oh, first to Washington, D.C. and then on to Russia, I guess you have to meet with the President first," *joked Russell.*

"Why, yes, as a matter of fact."

"Jesus Peter, who are you? You're definitely not the brother I've known all my life?"

"Russell, it's my charm. What can I tell you?"

Everyone laughed again.

Peter and Jenny said their goodbyes and left to go back to Peter's to relax before the wedding that afternoon. Every person in the kitchen was thrilled. Yes Jenny was everything a man could ever dream of, but that's not the reason they were so happy. It was because Peter was moving on with his life. Jackie would never be forgotten, but Jenny was truly welcome in their world.

They stopped by the hotel so Jenny could get her clothes. She decided to check out knowing she wouldn't be returning to the room that night. Plus she wanted to spend the remaining time that night and next day until her flight with Peter.

*   *   *

The ceremony went off perfectly as well as the reception. The party was breaking up and, even though Jenny was having a wonderful time, she wanted to leave. She knew this was the last night she would be with Peter and she was anxious to spend some alone time with him. Naked.

They barely slept again for more reasons then one. The other reason was that there was a lot of talking going on too.

"What are the chances you can visit me when I'm in Washington? I do spend a goodly amount of time in D.C."

"What did I tell you about the rumors and innuendo that sometimes surround me. I just don't want to put you in a compromising position."

"I don't care."

"I do, Jenny. You are a very important person."

"Right now the only important person in the world to me is you."

"If I can squelch some of the rumors, maybe. That's all I can say."

"Maybe isn't good enough. What about coming to Russia. I have a lovely place in St Petersburg and I can get time off over there. I kind of make my own schedule."

"That sounds great. I think that's doable."

Just exactly what Peter wanted when this whole thing started and now he didn't know what to do? He had to fulfill his end of the deal with Sotto to get out of the Mafia. He just didn't know what he was going to do.

The parting at the airport was a bit somber. There were tears. And Jenny cried too. That's how Peter described it to his family when he saw them next.

But the truth is the kiss as they parted was long and deep and neither of them cared who was watching. They were both saddened as she grabbed her briefcase to go to the gate.

"This isn't goodbye sweetheart. We'll be seeing each other soon. I don't know when or where, but it will be soon," said Peter.

Just before she left she whispered in his ear, "I love you."

Peter, in his usual way, whispered back, "Ditto."

She laughed one more time and turned to walk away. Peter reached out and grabbed her hand and kissed her again and said, "I love you too."

Peter turned to walk away. He was a different man than he was less than a week ago, but he wasn't sure he could do anything about it.

Peter needed help. He had to call a friend, someone that would do anything for him.

"Orin, it's Peter."

Major Orin Olsen was Special Forces Green Beret and the leader of the five-man Green Beret stealth unit that Peter, along with Nigel (Nitro) Burk, Joseph (The Cat) LaVaca, and Thomas (William Tell) Tully, was part of in Vietnam. These men saved each other's lives so many times you couldn't count them on two hands. They were brothers in arms and there wasn't anything that they wouldn't do for one another. Captain Olsen, now Major Olsen has been stationed at Fort Bragg, North Carolina and is the head of Intelligence there.

"Peter, you are not going to believe me, but I was minutes away from picking up the phone and calling you. Great minds think alike."

"You were, is something wrong?"

"Not at all. I was calling to tell you that Nitro is stateside. He's got some leave time, so he's stopping here at Bragg this weekend. I was calling to see if you wanted to join us."

"Hell, yes. When is he getting there?"

"Friday afternoon. He's coming in on a transport that's due to arrive at 1400 hours. I'll grab him when it lands."

"I'll be there and I'll be with you when you do. I miss you guys."

"Terrific! Did you just call out of thin air?"

"Not really Orin. You know the trouble I got in when I was hell bent on revenge?"

"Peter, of course. I'm still sick over what happened. Did the information I provided help?"

"That and then some. I got my revenge, but it turned out to be much more involved then I thought."

"Are you in a lot of trouble?"

"I'll explain when we get together. I don't want to talk about it over the phone. But if you can, I need a little more intel on another Russian guy."

"Peter, what the fuck have you gotten yourself into?"

"More than you can ever imagine, but with this information I think I can get myself out. Lock, stock, and barrel."

"What do you need?"

"I need everything you can get on a guy named Igor Terisenko. He's the head of the Russian Syndicate in Moscow. Everything your Intelligence Department has on him. We'll talk when I come there. It will be good to see you buddy."

"Peter, if you need anything else, Jesus I can't believe I'm saying this, but I mean anything, you know what I mean. I'll do it."

"Just the intel Orin, see you Thursday."

They had a wonderful reunion. Peter took Orin and Betty to the best restaurant in town and when he picked up the check he said, "I got this, no problem. Did I mention I'm rich?"

The next day the two friends stood next to the runway waiting for the third man of their five-man stealth force to land. Nigel (Nitro) Burke got off the plane with a smile you could hang your coat on. They hugged each other, very unmilitary like. None of them seemed to care.

"Jesus Peter, you look like a Goddamn movie star. Did you have a facelift or something?" said Nitro.

"Yeah, and I had my dick lengthened too. You want to see?"

All three laughed.

They were in a bar within 15 minutes.

"Where you stationed now Nitro," asked Peter.

"I'm in Germany. I hate it there. There's nothing to blow up."

They all laughed again.

"What about you Peter? How you been doing after, you know?"

"I'll never forget her. I came to realize that, even though it's been awhile now, I'm doing well. My business life has been good and I've come into some money so, all in all, I'm good."

Orin cut in, "He's fucking rich. The son of a bitch."

"Rich!"

"Shit happens," replied Peter.

Orin got serious for a moment and added, "Nitro, he got himself in some big time trouble."

"Orin, Jesus Christ. I didn't want Nitro to get involved."

"Involved in what. What happened? You need my help?"

"Peter, if one of us is in trouble, we all are. Maybe Nitro can help. Maybe he has a way of getting you into Russia. That's all I'm saying," said Orin as serious as a heart attack.

"Russia, Russia, what the fuck are you talking about?"

"Okay, but this goes without saying. This has to be between us. Period."

"Shut the fuck up. Who do you think you're talking to?" said Nigel.

"I know Nigel, but this is some bad shit. I think you know the story of how Jackie was killed."

"Of course, Peter. I was overseas or you know I would have been there."

"Stop, of course I know. Well the Russian bastard that machine gunned that Bagel place and took my Jackie from me was in the Russian Mob. Bottom line, I took him and the rest of those pieces of shit out. All of them and I got away with it."

"Good fucking deal. I hope you made them suffer."

"Well, the main man who runs the organization from Russia has put a hit out on me. I've killed the first two guys who tried so far, but I'm sick of looking over my shoulder. I plan on going over there and taking out this guy and whomever else I need to. How's that for a holy shit?"

"Holy shit."

"Right," added Orin.

Nitro added, "So you need us to go over there with you to kill a bunch of guys. That ain't going to be easy Peter."

"No, Nigel. I don't want you involved anymore than even knowing this shit. I just needed intel from Cap, I mean the Major. And, as far as getting in, I have an in."

"Who, what, how?" asked Nitro.

"Jesus, that's a lot of questions for three words. But anyway here it is. I met someone. I never thought in a million years there could be anyone else in my life, but this woman is something special she's a United States Ambassador. We hit it off and it has become serious, very serious."

"That's wonderful," said Nigel.

"That's where the "in" comes from. As much as I don't want to get her involved and I mean in the least, she's my in to Russia. She's the U.S. Ambassador to the Soviet Union. I can get a visa to visit her, take those cocksuckers out, and I'm free and clear and all of a sudden, I'm Peter again. I think I can start a new life with her. I can't believe I'm saying this, but I really love this woman guys."

"Happy for you there buddy," said Orin.

"Thanks. Here's another problem. I haven't been able to figure out a way to get a weapon over there. I'd love an assault rifle, but HOW?"

Orin interjected, "I can't help you their pal. Don't know what to tell you."

"I do," said Nitro. "Fuck shooting them. Blow the motherfuckers up."

"Yeah, I'll just bring a couple of sticks of dynamite on the plane with me."

"What the fuck, you know who you're talking to. I'll fix you up a solution that fits in a toothpaste tube. Stick a detonator in a small box of fuses cause it looks like one. You can stick that right in your luggage and then all you need is a pager. You stick everything under there car, call the pager, it blows, no collateral damage, and you're out of there with no one the wiser. Try and kill a friend of mine aye, and this is what you get. What do you think?"

"Perfect. But do you guys know what you're getting yourselves into?"

In unison they said, "Go fuck yourself."

Peter left Fayetteville with three things. From Orin, the intel on Igor Teriseko, which included addresses of where he lived, where his office is located, where he has lunch every day, and who his right hand man is. Orin had included pictures of Terisenko and of Yuri Mantanko, the next in line, and pictures of Terisenko's office and his home. From Nitro, he got an emptied-out tube of toothpaste that was then filled with enough explosives to blow a car to smithereens. It was safe to transport because it needed a detonator in order to blow. Plus he could carry it right in his toiletry kit. Thirdly, he left knowing that he had two guys that would walk into hell with him no matter the reason. This was starting to look possible.

Next, was the hard thing for Peter.

"Jenny, hi it's Peter."

"Hi, Oh my God it's good to hear your voice. I'm so happy you called."

"I had to. I miss you too much."

"Me too. You know it's only 9 weeks and we'll see each other. But who's counting?"

"Well. I can't wait 9 weeks. Any chance you can get some time off over there. It's only a 17-hour flight. I can do that standing on my head."

"God yes. Oh Peter, I love you. You know that right? Oh no, here it comes, I can feel it."

"Ditto," he said jokingly and continued with, "There I said it, I didn't want to disappoint you. But I really do love you too Jenny."

"When can you come?"

"ASAP. But I think I need a visa."

"Yes, you do, but I'll take care of that. Just fax me over a copy of your passport. All the information I need is on that. I can get you a visa in a day or two."

"Fantastic. I'll book a flight as soon as I can. I'm not kidding. I am missing the hell out of you."

"I can't wait sweetheart. This is the best call I've gotten in a long time."

"Give me the number to fax it to and I'll see you before you know it. Bye sweetheart, I love you. I said it first this time," said Peter.

"Jenny answered with, "Ditto."

Peter hung up the phone with the biggest feeling of mixed emotion he had ever had. He wanted to see this woman, that was never truer, but he felt like he used her. It was maddening to him. Peter realized what he was doing was for the two of them and it had to be done. He wanted to make it up to her, but didn't know how. Then it struck him.

Peter needed a ring.

Peter booked the perfect flight to St. Petersburg. All he thought about was Jenny. The Russian scumbag that was trying to kill him was almost a second thought to him.

If Peter was honest with himself, he would have preferred not to do what he had to do, but like any war, you fight and kill to protect, bottom-line for Peter, either Terisenko died, or he did.

Peter's plane touched down at 6:45AM Moscow time. His connecting flight to St. Petersburg wasn't until 9:00 PM. He had plenty of time, but no time to waste, before you knew it, he was flagging down a cab.

He waved one down and just said, "Lenin's Mausoleum."

Lenin's Mausoleum is situated in the heart of Red Square, the height of American tourism. Peter knew he could get lost in that crowd. Orin's intel showed Teriseko's office was just on the edge of the square so Peter felt safe taking a cab. An American going to Red Square is absolutely commonplace.

Donned in a mustache, sunglasses, and a baseball cap, he strolled in the direction of Teriseko's office. Peter decided to light him up like a Roman candle right in front of his office. A shinny new black limousine pulled up and parked in the alleyway next to the office. Igor Teriseko and Yuri Mantanko, Terisenko's right hand man, departed the vehicle and headed to the office's back door.

Peter waited a short while to let them settle in to whatever they were going to do inside. . He drifted over to the back of the limo and, pretending to tie his shoe, inserted the toothpaste tube bomb loaded with a detonator and attached pager in between the frame and the gas tank of the gagster's limo. It took but seconds to do that.

From there he dropped a letter in a nearby mail box addressed to whom it may concern with Terisenko's office address on it. It was a warning and the last warning the Russians were going to get. They weren't that stupid. This was enough warning to keep them in Russia. He then meandered over to a bench that had a perfect view of the parked vehicle and was situated right next to a phone booth and he waited. It was 11:10AM Moscow time. At exactly 1:00PM, Terisenko and Mantanko exited the building and jumped in the limo. Orin's information is that he went to lunch around then everyday. Orin was right. Mantanko started up the limo and Peter called the pager. **BOOM**, the blast rocked both of the buildings that the limo sat between, but no damage was done to either.

Teriseko and Mantanko were no more. Good riddance. Peter was free.

He headed back to the airport.

He landed at 11:20 PM St. Petersburg time. Jenny's smile lit up the entire gate. She waved and yelled, "Peter, Peter, I'm over here."

"You look more beautiful every time I see you."

"Peter how could this possibly be? We've known each other for such a short time."

"I felt this way towards you the first time we met with Bob for lunch. Jenny, I swear I really didn't want to. I told myself that the moment I saw you, but I couldn't help it. You are beautiful inside and out. You killed me right there. I tried to be cool, but I know I failed."

"Bob told me that I was really going to like you. He built you up so big I just knew you were going to look like Danny DiVito from that TV show Taxi, then I saw you."

Peter actually burst out laughing.

"Plus I couldn't believe it, you actually made a move on me. Guys do not make moves on me. You did, and here we are. The crazy thing is, I'm 15 minutes from ripping your clothes off."

"I'm not a play thing you know," Peter said almost laughing and they kissed right there in the bar. They left their drinks.

The next day was great and the night was magical. Peter had the ring ready, but he was going to wait for the right moment. He was petrified that she might say no.

They took the two-day bus tour of the city and Jenny saw St. Petersburg like she had never seen it before. She worked most of the time so sightseeing was not on her schedule.

There were only two days left before Peter was going home. Everything was perfect so far. The news announced that two known members of the Russian Syndicate were car bombed in Moscow by a feuding competitor. No mention of America. So first things first, Peter called Tony Sotto.

"Tony, the war is over. Terisenko and their number two guy, Yuri Mantanko, are dead. I left a warning for the next guy, as if their deaths weren't warning enough, that said: we can find you anywhere, stay out of America and we'll stay out of Russia. I signed it The Flower Man. It's done."

"That's good news Conti. I knew you would take care of this. The boys and me talked over what we discussed. You did everything you said you would do. We're making a lot of money over here and now the Russians are out, no competition. We are all sworn to secrecy and The Flower Man is dead. Thank you, Peter, **You're out.**"

"Wait Tony, one last thing. In the bottom left hand drawer of the desk, there's the deed to the Delaware Grill. I signed it and made it out to you. It's a gift from me to you for all you've done for me. Thank you, Godfather, and goodbye."

He did it. He was out. One thing down, now for the second, and he was scared.

That evening Peter and Jenny were walking along the Moika Embankment, a stoic walking area in the City, headed to the bronze horseman's statue of Peter the Great, the founder of the City. They sat on a bench admiring the beautiful statue when all of a sudden Peter said, "Jenny, you have changed my life."

"Both of our lives have been changed."

"Let me finish, I know we haven't known each other all that long and I know you love your job." He continued with, "But do you think it would be possible to just leave everything behind? I mean everything. Here's the thing, I bought a beautiful Villa on the Amalfi Coast. It's magnificent. What I'm saying is, I love you Jenny!" Peter reached into his pocket for the ring and said, "Jennifer Taylor Grier, WILL YOU BE MY WIFE?"

Jenny looked down at the beautiful ring and hesitated for a second. She had been waiting for this moment her entire life. The right man just never came along and now he has. She started to cry. They were happy tears, tears of joy. She took a deep breath, looked up at Peter, and just said, "**YES**."

*   *   *

Now Peter sits drinking coffee at a café in St. Petersburg Russia waiting for his fiancé to come out of her meeting. What's next for Peter and Jenny, God only knows.

IT'S A CHANGE OF LIFE.

CONTI III
Change is Coming

Chapter 4

Jenny met Peter at the café and sat down for a cup of coffee with her husband to be. She was one happy woman and it showed.

"Hi, handsome."

"I'm sorry, have we met?"

"Yes, you gave me this ring last night."

"Sorry, I forgot. I give one of those to a woman every night, but none as beautiful as you. I love you, you know."

"Ditto."

Peter just smiled and said, "You stole my line."

She bent over and kissed him.

"How was your meeting?" he asked.

"Well, I'm glad you asked. It was perfect."

"What do you mean?"

"They accepted my resignation."

"WHAT?"

"I'm getting married and I want to spend the rest of my life with my husband starting right now."

"Jenny, we had this conversation. You're a very important person to our country."

"Peter, I've served in the Congress and now as an Ambassador. I've done my share. I want to be with you."

Peter just smiled and reached out for her hand. "How does all of this work?"

"I'm going back to the states with you. I have to formally submit my resignation in Washington and debrief. Then sort of train or at least fill in my predecessor on the happenings here in Russia and then basically I'm out."

"How long will that take."

"Not long. President Fowler will appoint my predecessor almost immediately. I'll probably fly back here with him or her and introduce everyone to each other and fly home."

"Where's home."

"Wherever you are," she said with a smile that was so big it lit up the area.

"We have a lot to discuss then," answered Peter.

"Like what. The logistics really don't matter to me. I love you, you know," she answered.

"Ditto," he said with a smile.

They both laughed.

"I'm serious. What do you want me to do," asked Peter.

"Up to you. I guess you have to go back to Buffalo to your businesses."

"You guessed wrong. I resigned. Well, at least I retired. I have a new job and she's sitting right across from me."

"How can you do that?"

"Easy. I already made the call. I just have to cash out and I'm retired. Money is no object in our lives. We'll do something, but right now I don't care what it is as long as we do it together.

"You are making my head spin."

"I know what I'm doing. It's just that I don't care what we do. My life is you."

"You are smooth Mr. Conti. But there is no need for more lines."

"I've never been more serious in my life."

She just smiled and said, "I've never been happier."

"Jenny, there are decisions that have to be made now though, like where we are going to live and when. You have a place in Washington and a place here. I have a place in Buffalo and a place on the Amalfi Coast. What do you want to do?"

"Jesus Peter, I haven't even given any of that a bit of thought. I guess all of that is up to you."

"No way. You are not putting that on my shoulders, but if you want my opinion, I'll give it."

"Well?"

"Okay, let me start out with two questions. When do you want to get married? And do you want to live together before we do?"

"Easy. I don't care and yes."

"Nope, I need real answers."

"Those are real answers. As long as we're together, I don't care when we get married. There, I answered both questions with one answer."

"Jenny, you're killing me. I need answers, like, do you want to live at my place, your place in Washington, or the villa in Italy?"

"Yes."

"What kind of answer is that."

"It means I don't care where as long as were together."

"We're getting nowhere fast, so I guess I'll have to decide. How does this sound? I'm assuming you will have no problem getting out of whatever your deal is with the place over here. Do you own it?"

"No Peter, it belongs to our government. I'm sure my replacement will take it over."

"There, one thing out of the way. Do you own your place in D.C.?"

"Yes."

"Lock, stock, and barrel?"

"Yes."

"Okay, let's keep that, you never know?"

"All right. So far it seems like you have some idea on what to do," she said.

58

"That's right lady. I'm extremely intellements."

Jenny just laughed. "No really Peter, I want to hear your plan."

"It's not a plan. They're just suggestions."

"Then continue."

"Well, I do have a nice home in Buffalo where we can stay until our nuptials."

"What are nuptials?" she joked.

"Shut up and let me finish. My idea would be to stay in Buffalo and get married there, whenever you want. The sooner the better for me, but if you want a giant shindig; I'm fine with that. Something like that takes a little time though. Our families and friends are there so that makes sense. Once we get that out of the way."

"Stop. Out of the way?"

"I mean, once that beautiful day happens, I was thinking we could honeymoon in Italy for let's say a couple of years. How does any of that sound?"

"Doable. But we need to discuss it a little more I think."

"Well, let's hear your ideas."

"I just want to marry you and I don't care where we live."

"NO HELP WHATSOEVER."

Jenny just smiled and said, "If you want, I'll stay at your place."

"You know what I love about you, besides everything, is how you make things sound like they're my ideas when all along you knew what you wanted and tricked me into saying whatever that is in the first place."

"That's not true. I only wanted to honeymoon in Italy for a month or so."

Peter just laughed.

He really loved that woman.

CONTI III
Change is Coming

Chapter 5

They left the café and headed to what St. Petersburg is truly famous for, the canal tours. St. Petersburg is known as the Venice of the north. It's magical when viewed from its canals. The City was the vision of Peter the Great who built the canals by using the deltas of the Neva River. When you have as many canals as St. Petersburg, you have plenty of bridges; St. Petersburg boasts of 320 bridges and all are simply beautiful.

The City of St. Petersburg was founded in 1703 and was considered the gateway to the west. Historically significant sites clutter the banks of the canals as well as a number of historic museums. The City was Russia's capital until 1918; it's still considered Russia's cultural heart. The lovebirds were on their way to enjoy a beautiful day. They would be leaving this historic city, and Jenny her position, in a day or two. Peter wanted to see as much as possible. It's a magnificent place.

After a spectacular tour, the duo headed to a restaurant that is known as one of the top ten stroganoff restaurants in the world, The Palkin.

It was delightful and to Peter it was the end of a perfect 24-hour period of time.

"Sweetheart, I don't want to put a damper on anything. Today was absolutely flawless but I'm leaving in two days, so we need a plan," said Peter.

"Well, as I mentioned, I need to go back to Washington to finalize things. I guess after I'm finished, we'll have to make a plan then."

"Nope. I'm not leaving you. You might change your mind."

"Fat chance Mr. Conti. You already made me quit my job."

"You're blaming me?"

"That's right. You made me fall in love with you and turned my world upside down."

"Oh my God, you are blaming me," he said with a giant smile.

"I wouldn't call it blame. Magical is the word I would use."

"Stop right now. Here comes another manipulation, I can feel it."

"WHAT?"

"Jenny, what's on your mind now?"

"Well, since you don't really have to go back for work."

"Spit it out."

"Well."

"Just ask. I can feel it coming."

"What say you to accompanying me back to Washington while I get the paperwork and such out of the way. You know this engagement ring makes you my consort and makes D.C. accessible to you. I could introduce you to the President."

"Just tell me what you want me to do and don't try and bribe me."

"OK, what about we travel to D.C. together. Then together we come back here to Russia for my exit obligation and then, go to Buffalo. You could help me, and I have a lot to do before I can uproot my life."

She continued with, "Plus I really don't want to be apart from you. You could change your mind."

"Why do you always have to spin my words?" he said almost laughing. "Yes sweetheart. I will do whatever you need me to do. Your wish is my command."

"Peter, I love you and don't say ditto."

Peter answered with, "I wouldn't dare. This is too important. And I love you too much for jokes right now. Let's go back to the apartment and make the reservations. I'd go to Timbuktu with you if you asked."

"Where's Timbuktu?"

Peter laughed out loud.

The next thing you know, they were on a plane headed for Washington, D.C. and as soon as they landed Peter was on the phone.

"Mom, I did it and she said yes!"

Tears of joy slid down her face as she said, "I am so happy for you both my son. Tell me everything."
"I will Mom when I get home, but that won't be for a while. Jenny has a bunch she has to do here in D.C. and then we're heading back to Russia to finish things up there. She's coming home with me."

"Wonderful, wonderful news. Can't wait to see you both. I love you son."

"I love you too Mom."

THAT WAS THAT. CHANGE IS COMING. PETER CONTI IS STARTING A NEW LIFE.

CONTI III
Change is Coming

Chapter 6

Peter didn't want to admit it, but he was excited as he walked into the tunnel leading from the ally entrance on the south side of H Street NW and Vermont Ave, the business offices of the White House, to the White House itself.

Jenny had mixed emotions as she handed in her resignation to President Fowler's Chief of Staff Mark Stephens.

'I accept you resignation Jennifer, but it's with a sad heart. You have done a standup job and you will be sorely missed," said the powerful man.

"Thank you, Mark, I have always appreciated the confidence you and President Fowler have shown in me. It's just that, well let me show you the reason. Peter, Peter, could you step in here for just a minute?"

Peter walked into the influential man's office from just outside in the corridor to stand next to Jennifer.

"Chief of Staff Mark Stephens, I'd like to introduce my fiancée, Peter Conti. Mark, this man is the reason for my resignation."

Peter stuck out his hand and shook the hand of the very important man. "Sir, this is a pleasure."

"Peter, I would be angry with you if it weren't for the happy look on Jennifer's face. The pleasure is all mine."

With that, the most powerful man in the free world, President George R. Fowler, entered the office.

Jennifer, I wanted to take a second to say goodbye and to thank you for your fine work, both in Congress and as our Ambassador. You truly did stellar work and you will be missed. Is this the man that's taking you away from us?"

"Yes sir Mr. President. This is my fiancée Peter Conti."

Peter was near speechless when the President of the United States of America stuck out his hand to shake his.

"Mr. President this is such a great honor for me, but just so you know, it wasn't my idea for her to resign, I swear. But you know Jennifer, once she makes up her mind there is no changing it," said Peter with a giant smile.

"No need to explain Peter. I do know this woman, and you are dead right," the President said laughing. "By the way, it's not like we were spying on you, BUT there was a little checking up on who was stealing Jenny from us and sir, thank you for your service."

"It was an honor serving my country Mr. President."

"Well, you did a hell of a job soldier." He hesitated for a moment, but just before he turned to go back to the Oval Office he said, "One thing is for sure, we're leaving her in some very capable hands. Good luck you two."

In unison Jennifer and Peter both said, "Thank you Mr. President."

And like that he was gone.

The Chief of Staff gave Jenny her instructions on who she needed to debrief on the happenings for the transition and asked if she would be able to meet with her replacement for lunch on Friday. The new Ambassador was to be Margaret Hixson the ex-Senator from the State of Missouri.

"Of course, Sir. Will I be needed to go back to Russia with her?"

"No Jennifer. That won't be necessary at all. Actually, our Secretary of State, Thomas Pearl, will be accompanying her. It's already been arranged, but if you would like to join them, you certainly are welcome. George and I figured you probably are a little busy with everything right now," he said as he winked at the couple.

"Thank you, Mark."

"No, thank you Jennifer for the great job you've done and good luck to you and to you Peter."

Again, they answered in unison, "Thank you Sir."

They both shook hands with the important man and left. Peter, who doesn't get flustered at all, ever, was more than impressed.

"Honey, I am sorry. Are you sure you want to give up all this?"

"You just don't get it do you?" she said. And right in one of the hallways of the White House she kissed him.

Over the next few days Jenny was busy wrapping up a few loose ends, government wise, and Peter assisted with her personal chores. Basically, helping her get packed and prepared to change her life completely. He also did something, kind of behind her back just for a surprise for his future wife by arranging a going away party with a number of her friends and coworkers. Not everyone could attend due to the short notice, but there were still plenty of people who could make it.

Braden and Lainie Davis two of Jenny's closest friends were there. Anna and Andrew Cook also attended, Anna worked in Jenny's office and they became good friends over the years. Chase and Juliette Lamping made a showing. Juliette was Jenny's workout partner at the gym and her husband Chase worked in the executive office at the White House. Nancy and Tom Nord own the travel agency Jenny used and hence became friends through association. A number of her coworkers were there to say their goodbyes. Lisa, Matt, Jacqueline, Paul, Adrienne, and Jenny's assistant Dominic, all showed. Somehow Peter was able to contact these people and put the thing together in a very short time. It was a dinner at the swank LaBelle Restaurant in downtown Washington, D.C. Peter was able to procure the back room for the dinner party and it was a roaring success. Jenny was touched.

Jennifer Taylor Grier was a woman who was able to accomplish almost anything she set her mind to. She was strong, intelligent, hardworking, and successful, not to mention beautiful and talented. She was willing to give it all up, everything she had worked for, all for the love of a man. Peter wasn't about to let her down. On the contrary, he put her on a pedestal. This was a beautiful love affair.

They wrapped up everything Jenny needed to accomplish in Washington, and before you knew it, they were on their way to Mansion De Conti. That's what Peter called it when he jokingly bragged about it to his friends and family. In other words, they were on their way back to Peter's house. It was officially day one of their life together.

It was a happy day for both.

CONTI III
Change is Coming

Chapter 7

Hazel was pleasantly surprised when Peter walked into the house with Jennifer by his side.

"Welcome home sir," she said with a smile. "And it is especially good to see you miss."

"Thank you, Hazel, but I think you are going to see quite a lot of me for now on," she said as she showed Hazel her new ring.

"Well, bless my soul. I couldn't be happier for both of you. Is that all right for me to say?"

Jenny just hugged the woman. "Of course, we'll be telling everyone else in the family as soon as we get unpacked."

"Then you approve?" asked Peter.

"Sir, I'm elated."

"Hazel, Jennifer is not company so you can call me Peter in front of her."

"And it's Jennifer, Hazel. Not miss."

"I am going to make you the most special dinner tonight," she said with a giant smile.

"Put that on hold Hazel. Once I call my mother, there will be no way we're not eating there tonight."

"Congratulations to both of you."

In unison, they both said, "Thank you Hazel."

"One question Sir, I mean Peter. Will you still be needing my services now that you're getting married?"

Peter laughed out loud and said, "Hazel, you're part of the family and we couldn't live without you. So, the answer to your question is, of course. Nothing is changing except I won't be so grumpy all the time."

Hazel just smiled and giggled a little. Peter always made her laugh.

"What about lunch? Will you be staying for lunch? I will make you something extra nice."

Jennifer answered, "How about hot dogs?"

All three laughed and laughed. That was an inside joke for the three of them and made Hazel feel even more welcome. As previously mentioned numerous times, Jenny is a very smart woman.

They got settled in and once they were, Peter called his mother.

"We're back Mom."

"Dinner is at 6:00. Everyone will be here."

"Mom we just got in and the smoke hasn't even cleared yet."

"Dinner is at 6:00."

"Mom, Jenny."

Theresa Conti stopped him before he got another word out, "Peter, please."

"Mother, why do you know exactly what to say every time."

"Mothers know these things," she said laughingly.

Peter and Jenny laughed as well. Jenny was standing next to Peter and listening when he called.

The newly engaged couple arrived right on time. Peter's sister Marie was looking out the front window waiting for her big brother to arrive. Peter was hardly out of the car when Marie was hugging her brother and said, "I love you Peter, congratulations."

She ran around the car and gave Jenny a hug as well, "Congratulations, sis."

Jenny answered, "I can't believe this myself. I am so happy."

Peter's mom and dad and his sister-in-law Colleen were standing at the door to greet them as they walked in and there were hugs and congratulations all around.

Russell, standing a few steps behind the group, approached Jenny and said, "I have lost all respect for you Jennifer, how could you let this happen to such a beautiful and intelligent woman like yourself?" Then he hugged her and whispered, "I am so happy for both of you. Welcome to the family."

Peter was next in line for a hug from his loving brother. "Bro it's impossible to explain how happy everyone was when mom told us you two were getting married. You've always impressed me all my life Pete, but this here, wow. Congratulations my brother. I love you."

"Stop it all of you. I haven't even said yes to her yet," said Peter.

He got an expected slap on the shoulder from Jenny the second he said it.

Theresa had prepared an Italian feast for dinner. She truly outdid herself. Homemade ravioli, braciole (pounded flat round steak that is rolled up with hard boiled eggs, celery, and cheese inside, then tied together with string or with toothpicks and placed in the sauce to simmer for about four hours, along with the meat balls of course), a beautiful antipasto salad, and fresh homemade Italian bread. Even Peter's father Thomas had to pay his wife a compliment, the table when silent when he did.

"What, the meal was wonderful. Can't I pay your mother a compliment?"

Everyone laughed.

The conversation went to questions about Jenny's position as Ambassador.

"Well, I resigned. I have a much more important job now," she said with a smile.

Russell asked, "What did they say when you told them?"

Peter answered, "All I can say is when I was talking to President Fowler, he said."

"Oh, for Christ sakes. Stop right there," said Russell. "You met the President?"

"Yes, he was Jenny's boss, wasn't he?"

"Jesus Christ All Mighty, Jenny please tell us why in the world you are marring this guy. Please, we all want to know."

"I love him, that's why."

Peter stuck his tongue out at his brother like they did when they were kids, and everyone just laughed and laughed. It was perfect.

Theresa was making the after-dinner coffee when there was a knock at the back door.

"Come on in Sonny and Rose," said Thomas.

Sonny, Rose, Ray, and Kathy, Peter's best friends in the world, walked in with big smiles on their faces. Russell had called Sonny and told him Peter and Jenny were coming for dinner. They waited the appropriate amount of time, but Sonny was chomping at the bit to get there.

Sonny and Rose had already met Jennifer, but this was the first time that Ray and his wife Kathy had the pleasure.

"Had to come and congratulate you two," said Rose.

"Congratulations buddy, we are all so happy for you both," added Sonny.

"Damn, you're beautiful," said Ray. He got the usual slap on the shoulder from Kathy.

"What he meant to say is congratulations you two. Jennifer, I'm Kathy and this ignorant thing is my husband Ray. I think you've already met Rose and Sonny."

"Russell, go get the folding chairs. Sit down kids," said Theresa."

"We can't stay Mrs. C. We just wanted to congratulate our friend and his new wife to be," said Rose.

Thomas Conti, pointed to some chairs and, in his Italian father's way, pointed again and said, "Sit!"

The guys grew up with Peter, friends since grade school, so as soon as Mr. Conti said that, they sat.

Everyone in the room laughed.

The conversation was pleasant for all. Peter did a lot of the talking filing them in on his trip to St. Petersburg, but Jennifer filled in the rest, about her life in Russia and the happenings in Washington, D.C.

No matter who you were, you would have been impressed.

The fact is, everything that's happened over the last few years to Peter was difficult for them to even comprehend, but the love around the table was so evident that all of that just didn't matter. He was Peter and this was his new wife to be Jennifer. Nobody at the table thought that Peter would ever remarry. Knowing the way Peter loved Jackie, they all thought this was not possible because Jackie was such a big part of Peter's and all their lives, she was never, ever, going to be forgotten. But to see how happy Peter was, made all their hearts leap with joy. Jennifer was absolutely wonderful. Happiness filled the room.

Jenny was welcomed in such a way that she felt like she belonged, period. There wasn't an uncomfortable second when she felt like an outsider. It couldn't have gone better.

They left the joyous occasion and headed home. When they got in the car Peter asked, "How was that honey? Did you enjoy yourself?"

Jenny said nothing. She just sat there and cried, big tears of joy.

"What's wrong? Are you okay?"

"I'm just so happy. I love you Peter."

Jenny never really confided in Peter about her childhood. Jenny was an only child, who lost her parents to an automobile accident when she was but 15 years old. She moved in with her father's brother Frank and his wife Patricia who loved and took care of her until she went off to college. After that, she was on her own. She never really had a family like Peter's.

The warmth and love they showed one another, the compassion, and the true wear it on your sleeve caring for each other was something she never thought she would ever have in her life.

It only took a matter of hours.

But now, SHE DID!!

CONTI III
Change is Coming

Chapter 8

They got back to the house and just kicked back. It has been a crazy two weeks for them. Especially for Peter. Yes, his life was definitely changing and in ways Jenny would never know.

The next morning at breakfast the conversation turned to Peter's businesses.

"Peter, I don't really understand the I'll just cash out and retire concept. How can you do that?"

"Jenny, I am nothing but an investor now and I'd rather be out of any kind of decision making. I already made the calls I needed to make. I'm out." He continued with, "Sweetheart, money is no object in our lives. Just know that."

"Well, what are we going to do?"

"For a while, just enjoy ourselves. I mentioned Italy and I really want to spend some quality time there with you. I have an adopted family there and they are wonderful, wonderful, people. After we get married, I'd like to live there for a bit."

"I guess we need to discuss the getting married thing. I haven't really given much thought to things like the ceremony, the reception, and everything that goes with that. As far as being with you for the rest of my life, that has never left my mind. Not for a second. I am so happy Peter."

"I don't want to continue with the ditto thing. It was funny in the beginning, but now I just want to say, me too sweetheart." He continued with, "I'm overjoyed. I love you Jenny."

She responded with, "Ditto."

They both laughed a hearty laugh.

"Jenny, whatever you want, whenever you want, is my plan for our wedding?"

"Family and close friends and as soon as possible. How's that for a plan?" she replied.

"Not good. I want to show you off."

"You are so sweet."

"Don't you own a mirror? Take a look at yourself, you are absolutely beautiful."

"Peter, when are you going to stop with the lines? You already got the job."

"NEVER!"

"I love you, you know," she replied.

She waited for the ditto, but it didn't come.

Peter responded with, "AS DO I."

They laughed again.

Peter then asked, "What do you think about getting married in Delaware Park? It's a beautiful setting and we don't have to make reservations. Father James Nahorski, the priest at the Chapel at the Children's Hospital would surely perform the ceremony and I bet dollars to donuts Antonio would cater the shindig. Maybe even have it at his place."

"How can a man so handsome be so smart?"

"I read Dear Abby (the premier lonelyhearts columnist)."

Jenny burst out laughing.

"Oh, that reminds me. We better call Mayor Stonemetz. I think we owe him a debt of gratitude. Plus, we need to talk to him about the Children's Hospital charity program," added Peter.

"Let's go to his office and tell him in person," said Jenny.

"Great idea. Maybe he can fit us in for lunch?"

"Wait Peter, I have one more question. What favor did you do for the owner of Antonio's that he treats you the way he does? It must have been a pretty big favor?"

"It was something to do with his daughter Julie, sweetheart. Can we leave it at that?"

"You are too much Peter Conti. Too much," she said, but left it there.

Later that morning the happy couple headed over to see Robert Stonemetz at his office. Being the Mayor of Buffalo kept him on his toes and very busy, but he made the time to greet his friends and fellow charity partners.

"What is that on your finger Jennifer?" asked the Mayor with a big smile on his face.

"I lost the bet, so I have to marry him," she responded.

"That is such bologna Bob. The woman chased me for crying out loud." He hesitated a second and continued with, "Thank you Bob for introducing me to my future. I owe you pal."

"I knew you two would hit it off. I just knew it. Congratulations you two, really."

"Thank you, Bob. I couldn't be happier," responded Jenny.

"You have time for lunch?" asked Peter.

"I'd love to join you, but I have a previous luncheon engagement that I can't get out of. How about a rain check? I'm free on Thursday."

"That's a date," said Peter. "We can go over where we are with the charity."

"Boy, I'm happy for you two. Just thrilled. Congratulation!"

"Thanks buddy. We'll get out of your hair. You're a busy man. Which you keep telling me over and over again."

"SOOO."

Everyone laughed.

"How's Antonio's at noon?" asked Peter.

"I love when you say that. I love that place. Plus."

"Don't say it."

"I never have to pretend I'm going to pay," joked the Mayor.

They all laughed again.

The couple left and headed to Antonio's. Peter wanted to ask him about catering their upcoming wedding and maybe get a date from him. The park was always available.

They walked into the restaurant and there was Antonio Scavazzo at his usual spot welcoming Peter and Jennifer.

"Peter, so good to see you my friend and Jennifer, right? Nice to see you miss."

"Thank you Antonio," she said as she obviously flashed her ring at him and continued with, "I think you will be seeing more of me."

"Oh my. Congratulations you two. I am so happy for you."

"Thank you, my friend. Maybe later we can talk about a few things. You know catering wise?"

"I am honored my friend. Let's talk after you have your lunch. Pasquale, please escort Mr. Conti and his future wife to their table."

They sat and ordered drinks. Just as the drinks were being served, Peter looked over and saw two seedy looking characters escorting Antonio and his daughter towards the kitchen. One was holding Antonio by his arm. Peter rose quickly and said to Jenny, "Something's going on, stay here honey."

Peter was gone before he got the words all the way out of his mouth. He rushed to the windowed swinging kitchen doors and looked in. One of the guys was holding Antonio by his suit lapel. The other was standing next to Antonio's crying daughter Julie. Peter strolled in, like he was lost or something.

The man standing next to Julie shouted, "Get out of here. This is none of your business."

Peter held his hands up in the air and slowly walked towards the man that spoke to him and said, "Look Mr., I'm not looking for any trouble. I just saw you."

By the time he got to that point of the conversation, the hoodlum went for a gun. Peter kicked the man in the side of his knee so hard you could hear the knee break. At the same time, he grabbed the gun out of his hand and with the side of his other hand, swung it into the already incapacitated man's throat. He went down hard. Peter then, holding the hoodlum's gun, pointed it at the other scumbag and said, "Get your fucking hands off of him."

Peter walked over to where Antonio and this asshole were standing and pistol-whipped the man in his face. He went down. Julie ran to her father's arms.

"Go Antonio, take Julie with you."

Peter waited the few minutes it took for the bloody faced man to come to.

"Who are you and who sent you?"

"Fuck you."

That answer got him a mighty kick between his legs.

"I ain't going to ask you again. Who are you and who sent you?"

"Bill Jorgensen sent us," he said writhing in pain. "Who are you mister?"

"My name is Peter Conti."

"Oh shit."

"Look. Antonio doesn't need any more trouble here so I'm not going to call the police. However I can find out who you two are with a phone call, and if I have to do that, well I think you know what I'm talking about."

"Yes sir Mr. Conti. You'll never see us again."

"Good. Now you go back to Bill Jorgensen and you tell him that I said I want him to get out of this city, for good. If I hear he is still around in a week, people will call on him. If anything, and I mean anything ever happens to Antonio and anybody affiliated with him, Mr. Jorgensen will never be heard from again. Am I making myself clear? One more thing, tell Jorgensen the only reason he is still alive is because Antonio didn't want him dead. But I'm not Antonio. Tell him that too. Now pick up your friend and get out of here now. And use the back door.

The two men limp out.

Peter looked up and saw Antonio and Julie watching through the window of the door. So was Jenny. He walked out of the kitchen and Julie ran into his arms. She was crying hysterically.

"It's over sweetheart. Don't worry ever again. This is over. I promise."

She wiped her tears and said, "I love you Mr. Conti."

"I love you too Julie and you know how I feel about your father. This is over."

"Peter," said Antonio as he walked over and hugged him. "I have no words."

"It was that asshole Jorgensen. It's over. He'll never darken your doorstep again. Ever Antonio. You have my word."

"Thank you Peter. It's not enough to say just that, but thank you. You saved our lives."

"Antonio, that's what friends are for."

Peter turned to a frenzied Jenny. "Jenny, honey, hold on just a second, let's talk."

They sat back down at their table and Jenny excitedly said, "Oh my God Peter. Oh my God. What happened? Oh my God. Are you alright?"

"I'm fine Jennifer. Let me explain."

"Explain? Explain? Peter you were almost just killed. That man pulled a gun on you."

"Jenny, I had it under control. Honest sweetheart."

"You had it under control. What the hell were those men doing anyway?" She said, obviously near out of her mind.

"Okay. Okay. Calm down and I'll explain," he said calmly.

"You asked me this morning what I did for Antonio to treat me the way he does. That has everything to do with what happened today."

"How? Go on."

"Well, keep all of this to yourself, please for Julie's sake. A man named Bill Jorgensen sexually assaulted Julie and beat the shit out of her. The Scavazzos called the police, but to no avail. The man got away with it."

"What? What did you do Peter?"

"Hold on. Let me finish. Antonio came to me and asked for help and, before you even ask, not to kill the guy, but just for help. I'm a businessman. I used business tactics and I ruined the man, completely. He lost his business, and when that happened, he lost his wife. That's why Antonio treats me the way he does. Out of gratitude."

"Oh my God. That poor girl."

"Jorgensen hired these two hoodlums to pay Antonio a visit to retaliate for his loss. Like that asshole was the injured party. Thank God I was here. Do you remember the name Vito Bansano? I told you about his reputation and how he somewhat adopted me, right?"

"Yes. Vaguely, but yes."

"Vito was feared, let me put it that way. I just used his name to eliminate this from ever happening again. It's over. I don't expect you to understand this fully, but trust me honey, this whole episode is over."

"Are you sure Peter?"

"Absolutely positive."

"Jesus Peter. You are the bravest and toughest man I have ever met or have ever even seen in my life. Sweetheart I saw everything. My God honey."

"It's over. Period."

"Have I told you lately that I love you?" she said.

Peter just smiled.

CONTI III
Change is Coming

Chapter 9

They ate in silence. Peter was upset of course because his past just won't leave him alone. What Jennifer witnessed was fairly brutal and a little scary for her. She sat in contemplation and, after a short time, realized that what had just transpired was without doubt justified. Peter was nothing but protecting these people. He is a hero. That's what hero's do. Jenny felt relieved.

Peter was himself contemplating what just happened. Not about the two crooks he just battered, but that Jenny saw him do it. Would she be afraid of him now? He was worried sick about it.

"Jenny," he said. And that's all he got a chance to say.

Jenny cut him off and said, "No, Peter, I'm not afraid of you."

"I know honey, but what you saw me do."

"Was heroic. I feel safe around you is all you need to know."

"Are you sure?"

"Never more sure of anything in my life. I know your heart Peter, you might be really tough outside but inside."

"I am the luckiest guy in the world," he said.

"I know," was her answer.

They both laughed. Just then Antonio and Julie came over.

"Sit and join us," said Peter.

"Peter," said Antonio.

"Stop right there. No need to say anything. It's over. Everything since day one is over. Julie, you have nothing to worry about when it comes to that, excuse my language, piece of shit for a man. He will be leaving this city for good. That's a solemn promise honey."

"Mr. Conti. I don't know how to thank you."

"First off sweetheart, it's Peter, and just knowing this whole ordeal for you is over is all the thanks I need. You are special to me and you can come to me for anything, Okay."

Julie started to cry and Jenny reached over and put her arm around her. "Julie, I'm Jenny. When Peter says something like that, he means it. You and your father are safe. You can count on that."

The two women hugged.

Antonia spoke next. "Anytime you need anything from me, anything. I am in your debt my friend."

"Antonio, I already got what I need from you. Your friendship."

"Of course that goes two ways. Peter you mentioned before all this happened that you wanted to talk to me about catering. I am assuming you meant your wedding."

"That's right my friend, but now is not the time for such talk."

"Well, the answer is NO. I will not cater your wedding."

"DAD!" exclaimed Julie.

"Let me finish. I am going to close my restaurant whenever it is you want and your reception will be at Antonio's. It's my gift to you two."

"Can't let you do that Antonio," answered Peter.

"You have no choice. And that's that."

Jenny started to talk, but Antonio stopped her. "Jenny, may I call you Jenny? Please allow me and my daughter this privilege."

"Peter?" said Jenny looking straight into her fiancee's eyes.

Peter answered Antonio, "My friend you honor us and thank you, but not at your expense."

"Your money is no good here. So, don't make me fight you. I really don't think this old man could win."

Peter just smiled and said, "I know when I'm beat. Thank you both. We don't have a date, but we will soon."

"Done," said Antonio. "And do not leave a big tip today. You spoil my people."

Peter smiled and reached into his pocket and peeled off a number of big bills and said, "I won't, but here's a little something for you Julie. Today was a bad day for you sweetheart, I know how bad this entire ordeal must have been. So, here go buy yourself something nice."

Peter handed her a thousand dollars.

"No way. I can't. Daddy?"

"Peter!"

"Stop it you two. You have your way of saying thanks and I have mine."

"Take the money honey. He means that," said Jenny.

They all hugged. Antonio and Julie left the table and went back to their jobs. Peter and Jenny finished their meal. There was no bill as usual. Peter left a very hefty tip even though he said he wouldn't and they left.

"Well," said Peter as they got into the car. "When do you want to get married?"

CONTI III
Change is Coming

Chapter 10

Jenny hadn't decided as of yet the exact date to have the wedding. She hadn't even started looking at wedding dresses and invitations or flowers or entertainment etc. Peter just wanted to get married. Jenny needed some time to check these things out before even guessing a date. Help came to the rescue.

The doorbell rang and Hazel answered the door.

"Hello Mrs. Conti. Please come in. Peter and Jennifer are in the breakfast room having coffee. Would you like a cup?"

"That would be wonderful. Thank you."

"Follow me then. I'll bring that right to you."

"Ma. Hi," said Peter as his mother walked into where they were sitting.

"Hello Mrs. Conti," added Jenny.

"Jenny, as of right now, please call me Mom, Okay."

"Yes, Mom," said Jenny with a smile so bright it lit up the room.

"What brings you here Mom?" asked Peter.

"Jenny and I have a wedding to plan. What do you think I'm doing here?"

"So, you're saying you want me to leave?" asked Peter with a smile of his own.

Theresa Conti answered her son with a one-word answer, "Yes."

"I am mortified," said Peter. "And now I wish I knew what mortified meant."

All three laughed.

"You don't have to leave now son. I was only kidding. But Jenny and I have a lot to discuss and plan."

"I know Mom. Thank you. She has been whining like a little girl all morning."

"That is not true Mrs. Conti."

"It's Mom."

"That is not true Mom. I've only been whining half of the morning."

They all laughed again.

"Thank you so much for coming. I am so lost and Peter keeps nagging me about a date."

"I'm not nagging Ma. I may have asked a little too many times per hour, but I wouldn't call that nagging."

"Don't worry Jennifer. I know people who can help. The fact that you already have a venue for the reception is more than half the battle. Antonio's, wow."

"Now, Peter. How do I say this politely? Oh, I know. Get out!"

"I can take a hint. I've got places to go and people to see anyway."

"Thank you honey," said Jenny.

"You are so very welcome. I enjoy getting thrown out of my own home."

"Bye dear," said Theresa

"Mom, can I at least finish my coffee."

"Take it with you," she said almost laughing.

"I'm out of here. I can see I'm not welcome."

Peter did have a place he wanted to go. He was just building up the courage to go there. This was going to be hard, but he felt like he had to tell them himself before they heard it from someone else. Peter was going to his in-laws, the Millens, to tell them he was getting married.

*   *   *

He walked up to the Millen's front door with a solemn look on his face. Even looking at the house brought back memories that hurt him to the core. He loved Jackie with all his heart and her loss would stay with him forever. But as they say, life goes on. He just hoped they would understand.

"Peter, oh my, hello, come in," said a smiling Patty Millen.

"Thank you, Mom, is Mike home?"

"Yes, come on in and I'll make some coffee. Mike, Peter's here."

Peter hugged his mother-in-law and walked into the kitchen. Mike Millen had just gotten up from his chair to greet Peter when Peter walked in.

"Hi, Peter. What brings you here this beautiful morning?"

"I have some news that affects you and I wanted to tell you about it myself."

"What's the matter? Did something happen?" asked Patty.

"Well yes, but before I tell you I need to say something."

"What's the problem son," said Mike.

"Well, the thing is, I love Jackie and have loved her since I was nine years old. I will love her until the day I die. I know you know this."

"Of course, we do. You didn't have to tell us that," said Patty.

"I wanted to say that before I told you my news. So, here goes, I met someone."

"That's wonderful news," said Mike.

"Wait, there's more. I asked her to marry me."

"Congratulations son. That's great news. I assure you, Patty and I are very happy for you. Aren't we dear?"

"Of course, Peter. Tell us about her."

"Well you know I have been sort of rubbing elbows with some very high up people and during that process I met her. She was the United States Ambassador to the Soviet Union."

"Holly cow. How did you meet?" asked Patty.

"She is involved with the Children's Hospital Charity and we met through that."

"I'll bet she is a special woman," said Mike.

"She really is. She served in the Congress before her appointment as Ambassador. She is an intelligent, caring, beautiful woman. I never thought this could happen to me a second time, but it has. I debated getting into any kind of relationship with her but my mother, in her usual way, explained it as well as it could be explained. She said, If you were the one that left this world, would you want Jackie to stop her life and just mourn for you forever or would you want her to find happiness. Tell me son, what would you want for her? So, what do you think Jackie would want for you?

"That hit me hard. My mother is something else. I took her words of wisdom and it lifted me up. I truly believe Jackie would want this or I wouldn't do it."

"Peter, if you came here for our blessing, you have it. We love you son and we want you to be happy. You being alone will not bring our daughter back. It just ruins your life. Please understand we are truly happy for you," said Patty.

"Thank you. I don't think I could go through with this without this talk," said Peter.

Mike Millen stood up, put his hand on Peter's shoulder, and said, "It warms my heart to see you happy, both of our hearts. We love you Peter like you are our own son. This is happy news for us. This changes nothing with our relationship. Our whole family loves you and you will be welcome in our home forever and so will your new wife."

"You have no idea how that makes me feel. I love this family. I have always felt like a part of it and I always will. Thank you. I really needed this."

Patty switched the conversation by saying, "What's your fiancée's name Peter?"

"Jennifer Taylor Grier, Jenny."

"She sounds wonderful. Can't wait to meet her."

"I will definitely be sending the family invitations to the wedding. I don't know when that will be, but I wanted to personally invite you. If you decide you'd rather not attend, I understand, but you're family to me, so."

"We'll be there for you. We always will be there for you," answered Mike.

"Would you like some lunch Peter?" asked Patty.

"No thank you Mom. I need to get going. Will you inform Jill and Tommy? If they want to give me a call, they both have my number. When we send out invitations, we'll send theirs here with yours. The same thing as far as feeling about all of this goes for Jill too, of course. She might not want to come. If she doesn't, no explanation is needed.

"We'll all be there Peter, congratulations son," said Mike. Peter hugged them both and left.

CONTI III
Change is Coming

Chapter 11

On Thursday morning, Peter and Jennifer were headed to Antonio's to meet Bob Stonemetz for lunch. They arrived just in time to catch Bob getting out of his car, so they walked in together. Antonio, as usual, greeted them at the door.

"Welcome Mr. Mayor," said Antonio Scavazzo. He turned to Peter and gave him a hug. "My friend every time you and now your fiancée enter my building it is an honor for me."

"Stop with that. Can't I just come to my friends place for lunch?"

"Yes, but my gratitude will never end. You are welcome here forever."

As Pasquale led them to their table, Bob had to ask for the umpteenth time, "Peter, really, what did you do for this man?"

"Bob, can I just say an injustice towards his daughter needed to be resolved and I resolved it."

"That's a start but could you please be a little more specific?"

Jenny answered, "He resolved it once and for all physically Bob. I witnessed it."

Peter added, "Bob, I'm tougher than I look."

They all laughed, but the Mayor got the picture. Peter's reputation as a hero just raised its head again and the details were not important. Let's just say that Bob Stonemetz has a lot of respect for his friend Peter, and we'll leave it at that.

The conversation turned to their mutual charity. Peter missed the last board meeting when he was in Russia and Bob filled him in. All was well. They were near their goal for the year and everyone at the Hospital was elated with the contributions they were bringing in. Peter couldn't be happier. That went for everyone at the table.

"Tell me about your trip to Russia," said Bob.

"Well, I was a little surprised at how much crying went on after I asked Jennifer to marry me. But I was able to stop crying after a few minutes."

They all laughed again.

Peter continued with, "It was breathtakingly beautiful. St. Petersburg is chock full of history and Jennifer was the perfect guide. The fact that this beautiful woman agreed to marry me made it the best trip I have ever been on. Look at her will you Bob, isn't she one of the most beautiful women you have ever seen?"

Peter received the patented slap on the arm for that comment.

"Owww, you are going to break my arm one of these days!"

"Shut up you baby, but thank you honey, you are so sweet."

"Get a room will you two," said Bob.

They all laughed once again. These people were good friends.

The lunch was great as usual and as usual there was no bill. Peter called Antonio over.

"My friend, thank you for your generosity, but this no bill thing is over. I won't come here if you keep it up."

"Peter, this place is my home. When you invite good friends to your home do you give them a bill after they eat?"

"Damn it Antonio, why do you say things I have no comeback for?"

"You can come here every day my friend. This is not payback for what you've done for my daughter and me. This is pure friendship."

Peter got up and hugged the man and secretively slid a number of hundred dollar bills in his pocket when he did.

"You are a good man Antonio. Thank you for your friendship."

Both Jenny and the Mayor saw him do it and just smiled.

This time it was the Mayor who left a hefty tip on the table, and they left.

CONTI III
Change is Coming

Chapter 12

Peter's mom and Jenny made phone call after phone call and were able to lock down a date. They could pull the entire thing together in 10 weeks. That put the day of the wedding on Sunday June first. Everyone would have preferred it to be on a Saturday, but Jennifer, knowing the loss of revenue for Antonio to shut down his restaurant on a Saturday, thought it would be too much to ask. His generosity was already overwhelming, and she felt it would be asking just too much. Sunday would be fine.

Peter walked into the kitchen just as his two favorite women in the world were finishing up the paperwork.

Jenny smiled at Peter and said, "How would you like to be my husband on June the first?"

"June the first. Can't. I was planning on straightening my sock drawer that day."

Jenny couldn't reach, but his mother was able to and gave Peter the patented slap on the arm.

"Sorry, honey. I meant to say, any day and time would be the right time for me. If June one makes you happy, I'm happy."

Jenny jumped from her chair into his arms and they hugged a hug of joy. Peter's mom just smiled.

Jenny added, "There are just a few very minor details I need to accomplish, starting with asking Gwen to be my maid of honor. Peter, I was thinking of having a very small engagement party for my girlfriends in Rochester, maybe a luncheon. Would you mind coming?"

"When did you want to do it?"

"I was thinking this Saturday."

"Sure sweetheart. That would be nice. Do you have a place in mind?"

"Well, Gwen works at the Marriott right there in Rochester and I'm sure she can get us a reservation in the dining room. Lunch time is never super crowded."

"That would be nice," said Peter. "Sounds like a plan. Are you going to ask them to bring their husbands? It would be nice if I wasn't the only guy there, plus your girlfriend Gwen's husband Joe and the other guys are great. I like them a lot. We hit it off nicely at Gwen and Joe's wedding. It would be good to see them again."

"I didn't think about that, but sure. The more the merrier."

"Great set it up."

"Have you thought about a best man, honey?"

"Sort of, I almost have to ask Sonny, but I want to talk about that with Russell first. I don't like to talk about the past, but Russell was my best man then."

"I'm so sorry Peter. I didn't mean anything by that. I wasn't thinking."

"Stop right there. Jennifer, God took Jackie away from us. It left a giant void in my life, no doubt, but God works in mysterious ways and, along with pain, he also brings joy. I never thought I could love like that again, but then you came into my life. I love you with every inch of my being. Never, I mean never think anything else. We were meant to be together. I feel that in my heart. Why it happened just doesn't matter. It has been magical from the first second I laid eyes on you. It's you and me for the rest of our lives," he said and hugged her and held her longer than usual.

Theresa Conti wiped the tears from her eyes and said, "That was so beautifully said Peter. Jenny, I know my son. Don't ever doubt what he just said, I'm sure of it. You know why I'm so sure? He said that in front of me, that's why. Wow, he must really love you sweetheart, I mean really love you. Saying something like that in front of me is NOT like my Peter. At All."

Jenny hugged Peter again and whispered, "I love you Peter, more than you could know."

Peter answered, "I said it first." And then they kissed.

*   *   *

Peter and Jenny walked into the Rochester Marriott right on time.

Gwen, Georgette, Frankie Ann, Karen, and Judy and the other Jenny, Jenny's lifelong friends were standing there waiting and when Jenny walked in, they cheered. Peter skirted the ladies as they all hugged, and he headed to the big table where the guys were sitting.

Joe stood up first to shake Peter's hand and Kurt, Rafael, Al, and Dan followed. Joe was the spokesperson and simply said, "Congratulations Peter. We're all happy for both of you. Seriously, you guys are the perfect couple."

"I'd love to make a joke right now, but guys I really hit the jackpot with Jennifer. She's perfect."

"No shit Sherlock," answered Joe. Everybody laughed.

Kurt interjected, "She didn't do too bad herself. Don't think for a second we don't remember your bravery the night before the wedding."

"Oh, that. Man, that cost me $500. Those guys didn't come cheap."

They all laughed again. But they saw Peter face off, and back down four hoodlums alone. Heroic was the word they all would use when they talked about it.

"It's good to see you guys. I thought I'd see you brother Steve, Joe?"

"He's out of town on business, but he sends his regards and his wife the other Jenny is here. He did ask me to make sure I congratulated the two of you."

"Tell him thanks from me and that I hope to see him at the wedding."

Just then the guys heard the squeal.

"Yes, of course. I'm honored," said an ecstatic Gwen, loudly.

Peter turned to the guys and said, "Jenny just asked Gwen to be her Maid of Honor."

"That figures," said Rafael.

"When's the wedding?" asked Dan.

"June 1. It's a Sunday, but it was the only day we could get Antonio's Resturante for the reception."

"ANTONIO'S! You rich bastard," joked Joe.

"That's right, but I'll be eating macaroni and cheese for dinner for the rest of the year."

"Yeah, right," added Rafeal.

Everyone laughed again.

The girls came over and there were hugs all around.

Gwen led the line of woman that hugged and congratulated Peter, while the guys were doing the same to Jennifer. It was a very nice time shared by all.

Joe tried to pick up the tab, but Peter made sure he took care of that before they even sat down. He gave the head waitress his credit card when they arrived, just in case.

"Peter, Jesus, this is our town. We were going to pick this up."

"Thank you all, but Jenny would have kicked my ass if I let you do that."

Jenny just smiled and shook her fist at Peter.

Everyone laughed again. It was perfect. Jenny was beaming with joy.

Now for the Best Man.

CONTI III
Change is Coming

Chapter 13

Peter was dealing with a small dilemma. His three life-long buddies were Sonny, Ray, and Al and all were deserving of the honor of being Peter's Best Man, but Russell was Peter's brother. Peter loved Russell that goes without saying and when he married Jackie, Russell was the one standing next to Peter serving as Best Man. Peter felt that one of the others should do it this time. He needed to talk to Russell.

"My brother," said Peter as he walked into Russell's office at his accounting firm unsurprisingly named, Conti Accounting.

"What are you doing here? You never come here."

"When will you get the hint that I don't like you?"

"I'm telling Mom you said that," Russ answered as he got up to hug his brother.

"Russ, here's the thing. You are an intelligent and understanding man, right?"

"Oh, shit. What did I do?"

"No Bro, it's nothing like that. It's just that you're a man and Sonny is a whining cry baby who thinks I'm going to ask him to be my Best Man at the wedding."

"Are you asking me if it's okay if you ask Sonny to be the Best Man at your wedding?"

"Russell, I love you brother and you are definitely going to be one of the groomsmen with Ray and Al, but Sonny will pout, and stamp his feet, and whimper if I don't ask him."

Russ just laughed. "Brother, I would be honored to be a groomsman at your wedding. Even though I'm so pissed off right now I can hardly contain myself."

"Does that mean you don't mind if I ask Sonny?"

"What is wrong with you? Do you actually think I would feel slighted if Sonny was your Best Man. I'm just so happy for you brother, that's the last thing on my mind. The fact that you're standing here right now and we're even having this conversation speaks volumes to me. I love you too Peter."

The two brothers hugged, and Peter whispered, "I am expecting a super big wedding present Russ. I'm just saying."

"Why do you always have to ruin the moment? This was something beautiful and you had to ruin it by bringing up something materialistic."

"Is that your way of ducking the gift thing?"

"Yes, it is," answered Russell with a giant smile.

"Thanks Russell. What I would like to see happen is to get the guys together and, if I can talk Sonny into inviting us all over to his place on the lake for a drunken fishing trip, that would be perfect. You want in?"

"Absolutely. When?"

"I'll call the baby up and try and set it up for this weekend."

"I'm in, no matter when it is."

"Great, I'll call you. See you later my brother."

"Bye Peter. It's so great to see you so happy. Call me to confirm the fishing thing."

Peter left and decided not to call Sonny; he headed over to Sonny's office instead. Sonny and Rose owned a small chain of dry-cleaning stores, Tonawanda Cleaners, and Sonny spent way too much time in the office overseeing the operation. Peter knew he'd be there and was going to talk him into going out for lunch. It didn't take much convincing.

"What's up?" asked Sonny as Peter walked into his office.

"Lunch?"

"Yeah."

That's how much convincing it took.

The two life-long friends decided to have lunch at the neighborhood bar they basically grew up together in, Jake's Bar and Grill.

Sonny started the conversation. "I feel like a question is coming," he said with a giant smile.

"Well, here goes, any chance me and the guys could go to your place on the lake this weekend for a drunken fishing party?"

"That's your freekin question? You dragged me out to lunch, for which you're paying for by the way; to ask a question you already knew the answer to? YES, OF COURSE. What the hell?"

"Oh, yeah, one more thing, would you be the Best Man at our wedding?"

"YES! OF COURSE! You are unbelievable you know that Peter."

"What do you mean unbelievable? We've been friends for 30 years for Christ sakes."

"It's not that I'm not honored that you just asked me to be your Best Man. It's just that I know you. You just asked me so I would pick up the check for lunch. You are so transparent Pete."

They both smiled and hugged.

The get together was set. The boys were all in. They met at Sonny's very nice weekend place on Lake Erie Saturday morning. The odds that it was going to be mighty drunk out that night were quite high.

Sonny has a very nice boat tied up at the dock that accommodated all five of them with ease, which included Sonny, Ray, Al, Peter, and Russell. Sonny stocked everything including the minnows, beer, sandwiches, and big cigars. All they need now are some fish to bite, small mouth bass and lake perch were the targets. They planned on a fish fry for dinner.

It was great. They were like boys again. Plus, they even caught fish. They cleaned their catch and headed back to Sonny's place.

"Did you even get a bite Al?" asked Ray.

"Kiss my ass, I was drinking beer."

"Is that anyway to talk to a friend?" asked Sonny.

"A friend. You think Ray and I are friends? I heard Peter ask Ray, do you hate Al? You know what Ray said? JUST HIS GUTS."

Everyone laughed and laughed.

Ray then said, "That is not true. You know I love you man."

"OH OH, it's getting drunk out already," said Russell.

Everybody laughed again.

They were sitting around, and beer turned to whiskey. After a number of shots Peter said,
"Guys this is important. I have a deck of cards here. I'm going to shuffle them up and give each of you a card. Here's where it's important. High card will be Best Man at my wedding and low card will be the groomsman."

"That sounds fair," said an all smiling, knowing Sonny.

"Now don't look at your cards until everyone has one, OK."

Peter handed out the cards. "Let's start with my brother. Take a look at your card Russ and tell everybody what it is."

Russell smiled as well same as Sonny but played along and said, "I have the two of spades."

Peter said, "Well shit. Can't get lower than that. I guess Russ is my groomsman. But high card is still out there. What do you have Ray?"

Ray turned his card over and smiled, "NOW WHAT Pete, I have a two also. The two of diamonds."

"Well so be it, said Peter. "I guess I'm going to have two groomsmen. That's only fair, a tie is a tie. It's down to you two, high card is my Best Man. Sonny?"

Sonny jumped in the air, but it was extremely poor acting. Peter just laughed.

"Ace of clubs?"

"Goddamn it. This is fixed. Why do I always have to get it broken off in my ass," said a pissed off Al.

"It ain't over Al. You might get an ace as well. What do you have?" asked Peter.

Al turned his card over and smiled. "You son of a bitch Peter."

"What is it Al?" asked Sonny.

"Two of hearts. This was a set up. All you bastards can kiss my ass."

They laughed and laughed.

"I asked Sonny the other day. He's the only one of you who would have cried if I didn't ask him. It was going to be you guys all along. I just wanted to have a little fun Al."

"FUN. You call what you just did FUN?"

"Yes," said Peter.

"It is kind of funny, I guess. Let's trick the one-eyed guy who lost his eye when he got blown up with a hand grenade in Nam, fighting for his country. That's kind of funny."

In unison they all said, "Kiss my ass Al."

Al just laughed. They all did. It was great.

It was settled. Peter had his wedding party all arranged, sort of. He needed ushers and he had that planned out too. They wouldn't be wearing tuxedos though. They would be in the dress blue uniforms worn by Green Beret.

Peter needed to make a few phone calls.

CONTI III
Change is Coming

Chapter 14

Peter rang the phone and Orin answered.

"Major Olson?"

"No."

"Orin, is that you?"

"Yes, but for your information, it is Colonel Olson now."

"Wow, congratulations buddy. Who did you have to sleep with to get the promotion?"

"Peter, I'm not gay, BUT $25.00 is a lot of money."

Peter burst out laughing and said, "Great news pal, you deserve it. Will you still be stationed at Fort Bragg?"

"Hell yes, I'm the commanding officer here now."

"News just keeps getting better and better."

"Thanks, BUT what the hell. I've been waiting for this call. I figured you were tucked away in a Russian prison or dead."

"Sorry buddy. I know I should have called sooner. The deal went off as planned. My problem is solved."

"How you get yourself in these messes is beyond me. I'm just glad it's over."

"Me too Orin, but on the other hand, I do have some very good news."

"Well, shoot."

"The woman I told you about over there in Russia. She's not there anymore. She quit her job when I asked her to marry me."

Orin put the phone down for a second and you could hear him shout, "Betty, it's Peter. He's getting married." He put the phone back up to his ear and said, "That is wonderful news, congrats buddy."

"That's why I'm calling. Any chance you and Betty can come up here around the first of June for the wedding."

"Hell YES."

"Great, any chance you would like to be an usher again?"

"Would love to."

"Do you know if Nitro is still stateside?"

"He is. In fact, he and Sally are spending the weekend with us before they head to Fort Dix. He's a major now. He's one of the foremost authorities on explosives in the country. Did I tell you that?

"I knew about his promotion, but him being recognized as the foremost authority, I didn't know. Great news."

"Back to the subject. Any chance you and your lady would be able to come as well?" asked Orin. "Betty and I would love to meet her and I'm sure Nitro and Sally would too."

"Hell YES." "Well hold on for one second." Peter laid the phone down and was back in less than a minute, "Hell YES."

"You had to ask, didn't you?"

"SOOOO."

They both laughed.

"I have to ask Betty too but I'm sure we're in for the wedding."

They both laughed again.

"Let me know what time your flight lands and we'll pick you guys up at the airport. This is great. I can't wait to tell Nitro."

"If you talk to him before me, tell him the wedding is June 1st and to bring his dress blues. You're both ushers. I won't take no for an answer."

"You won't have to Peter. Congratulations again. When you told us about her before you went over there, we both thought what the hell does she see in him, so you've done well my friend."

"She thinks I'm handsome. So there."

They both laughed again.

"I'll try to get there in the afternoon so we can all go to dinner. What time do you expect Nitro and Sally?"

"Mid-day Friday."

"Perfect. Just perfect. See you then Colonel."

"That does have a nice ring to it, doesn't it?" said Orin.

"It sure does Orin. See you Friday."

Orin, Betty, Nigel (Nitro), and Sally were standing at the gate when Peter and Jenny stepped off the plane.

Betty whispered to Sally, "Oh my God, she's beautiful."

Peter waved as they approached and immediately introduced everyone to Jenny.

Betty was the first to speak, "Jennifer welcome, Peter told Orin and Nigel you were pretty but goodness gracious girl, you're beautiful."

"What a wonderful thing to say Betty. Thank you. Did Peter put you up to saying that?"

"No sweetie, I have eyes."

Everyone laughed.

Nigel spoke next, "Nigel is my given name Jennifer, but Nitro is what I go by. My job deals with explosives."

"Jesus Nitro, here you are in the uniform of a Green Beret and you're called Nitro, do you really think you had to explain that," said Peter.

"Why, yes Peter. It could mean something else you know," he said using a proper English accent.

Everybody laughed again.

Next to speak was Orin. "Colonel Orin Olson at your service Mam."

"I knew you were going to bring up your rank. Why don't you say that over the loudspeaker so everybody in the airport can hear?" said Peter.

"Do you think that would be too much?"

Everybody laughed once more.

Sally spoke, "Jennifer, I'm Sally. Please excuse these men, every time they get together, they act like little boys. It's so embarrassing, but at least they're consistent."

"I don't know about that. They look pretty darn scary to me," answered Jennifer.
Then Betty said, "Yes, maybe these two galoots, but Peter looks like a damn movie star. Hi Peter."

"Thank you, Betty, finally someone said something to me."

Then Betty and Sally both hugged Peter and Betty said, "Congratulations you two, all of us our so happy about this. We love Peter. He's family to us."

"I don't love Peter. Do you Nitro?"

"No Orin. I do like him a lot though."

Peter retaliated with the middle finger salute and said, "There you go. And I was going to buy dinner tonight."

Orin came back with, "Now that I think about it. I do love you Peter."

"Me too," said Nitro.

Everyone laughed.

These three men had saved each other's lives so many times you couldn't count them. They put themselves in harm's way dozens of times doing it. When you fight alongside a man in war, a bond is formed that is difficult to explain. It's just there and there for life. These three along with Joe LaVaca and Tom Tully the other two guys in their highly decorated five-man Green Beret stealth unit, have that bond and would still walk into hell for each other.

"Wait, you're still going to buy dinner right Peter?" asked Nitro.

"I'll buy diner," said Jenny. "You're right Sally they are like little boys."

"Thank you, Jennifer, but I'm buying dinner," said Orin.

"Over my dead body," said Nitro.

"See what you started Peter," answered Jenny.

"All this dinner talk and all of a sudden I'm starving," responded Betty.

"So are we. What's the name of the place we ate at last time I was here?" asked Peter.

"Dominic's. Best restaurant in Fayetteville, North Carolina," answered Orin.

"Let's go there," said Peter. "Do we need to rent a car, and did you make reservations at a hotel for us?"

"First, you don't need a car. I have a Ford Expedition that seats seven. Second, you are staying with all of us at our place. Every time you visit you ask me that and every time, I say the same thing. Jesus, how many times do I have to tell you this stuff? And that's an order."

"Yes Sir," answered Peter.

Everybody hugged one another and they left for the restaurant.

The dinner was fantastic. The food was good too. You see, Jennifer had the group mesmerized with her resume'. After all, she did serve in the US Congress and was the United States Ambassador to the Soviet Union. Sally and Betty were just full of questions and Jenny answered them the best she could, without giving away any classified information of course. The guys were intrigued as well, not because of the depth of her resume', but that this absolutely beautiful, accomplished woman would somehow agree to marry Peter, not that Peter didn't deserve to have someone this great. Orin and Nitro had the utmost respect for their friend and confidante. Hell, they loved the guy. But this woman was perfect. All four of his friends were thrilled that Peter and Jenny found each other. They all could see them beaming when they looked at each other. This was a perfect match.

There was no fighting over the bill. Orin had given his credit card when he made the reservation. When Peter called for the check, Nitro threatened Peter with information that he would disclose to Jenny if Peter didn't let him have the check. Orin just smiled.

They enjoyed a number of after dinner drinks. The men especially partook in perhaps too many. So many that when they got up to leave Betty said, "Give me the car keys mister Olson." He did without argument. The six-some headed to the Olson's.

The night was just beginning.

CONTI III
Change is Coming

Chapter 15

The three Green Beret blood brothers sat in the family room drinking, and I mean large quantities of alcohol. The women were in the kitchen kibitzing and enjoying each other's company, when Betty got up to check on the men. She got halfway into the family room when she overheard something she had never heard before. The guys were talking about Vietnam. Something they did, only when they were together, never to anyone else.
Betty called the other women over to eavesdrop.

Peter started the drunk talk. "You guys saved my life so many times and I've never said thank you," said an intoxicated Peter Conti.

He got in unison, "Fuck you."

"No, I mean it. Remember when I got my ass blown up at the Tong River Bridge. Jesus Nitro."

All three women gasped when they heard that.

"You carried my sorry ass miles. I had no fucking idea where the hell I was, hell no doubt I would have died."

"Yeah, I nearly got a fucking hernia carrying your lard ass."

"Bullshit, the other three of us offered till we were blue in the face to take a turn, but this stubborn bastard wouldn't put you down. He kept saying this is my brother."

"That's a fucking lie. I wasn't saying brother, I was saying don't bother now that he got the shit blown out of him, he's not that heavy."

All three guys laughed.

"I'm not listening to that crap. Thank you, my brother," said Peter.

Nitro responded, "Do you have any idea how many gooks you killed when you were climbing them trees so we could crawl through the fucking jungle at Fong Lo Peak? Do you Pete? Jesus Christ, you shot one right out of a tree that was right over my head. Hell, he landed at my feet. He was about to cut my fucking throat."

"I thought that was Joe. If I would have known, it was you. Well maybe I would have still shot," said Peter laughing like it was nothing saving his friends life. "That reminds me, are Joe and Tell still serving?

Orin answered, "LaVaca's out. The guy is hard to get in touch with though. I tried to contact him to see if he could make it this weekend, but he's out of the country on business, I guess. Like I said he's sort of off the map. Tell, I mean Major Thomas J. Tully, is serving another tour in Bakstana. We talk occasionally but he's in the middle of nowhere so it ain't easy."

"Major aye, good for Tell. Where the hell is Bakstana anyway? It doesn't matter. I certainly want to invite them both to the wedding, but it doesn't sound like I'll have any luck with that. I'll mail invitations here with yours so at least they won't think I blew them off. I owe those guys. I owe you all. You all saved my life a bunch of times. At least I was able to pay you guys back a time or two."

"Bullshit," added Orin. "A time or two. Every fucking mission we were on you were there for us. That assault rifle of yours was our lifeline. When you dropped that gook out of the tree above Nitro, not five minutes later you saved my bacon. You remember Nitro. I thought I was so smart and slid down this embankment thinking we could cut off some distance that would give us a straight shot to be able to knock out the machine gun nests protecting the entrance to the peak. I slid down straight into two gooks camped at the bottom. I reached for my sidearm but didn't even clear leather when they both fell dead. Peter sniped them both from his position. What a fucking shot you are buddy."

The two wives and the future wife just listened in disbelief. These guys were talking about war like it was a high school game they all played in together. They were all decorated to the hilt with medals galore for the things they did there. As a Green Beret stealth unit fighting in Vietnam, they had no equals. They were the best of the best. Betty was crying. The girls got up to leave. They felt like they were spying, but they were so completely enthralled in hearing about their men's heroics it was like they were glued to their seats. Then Orin asked a question all three women wanted to hear the answer to. In fact, they all wanted to hear.

"Pete. We never really asked you how you got the handle PO JING PETE. I remember hearing it the day we met, but I knew you were green, so I didn't want to press," said Orin.

"Yeah Peter. The whole camp was talking about it."

All five of them listened intently as Peter started.

"The fact is, I didn't know what the fuck I was doing," started Peter. "I just got to Nam two days earlier. I got to DaNang and got orders to go to PoJing and report to a Captain Olson, well you were a Captain then Orin. Okay, that doesn't sound so bad I thought. Well on our way there, I was riding in a supply truck in a small caravan heading to PoJing when, all of a sudden, enemy fire pinned us down. Sergeant Myers was in charge and was driving the lead truck we were in. A bullet smashed the windshield and he was hit. I managed to grab the wheel and get us off the trail. I won't call it a road."

Again, the three women gasped.

"When he went down, me being the highest-ranking soldier, I took charge. I got Meyers out and huddled the other soldiers around him and said I wanted them to stay put. I was going to do some recon to survey our situation. Remember, I didn't know what the fuck I was doing, and I was scared shitless. But we were still taking fire, so I had no choice. I slithered towards where the fire was coming from. I knew the gooks were advancing towards the trucks on foot. I didn't hear any vehicles. I ran smack dab into a bunch of them sons of bitches and somehow killed them all. Now I was in the middle of the whole shooting match, but the shots were still coming from the snipers. I made my way through the jungle and luck stayed with me. I stumbled onto a few more of those bastards and I got them too. I finally got a position on the snipers and dropped them out of the trees they were shooting out of. Then on my way back, I hunted and found the remainder of the group still sneaking towards the trucks. When it was over, there weren't any left alive. I went back to the men and we headed to your camp. That was it."

"How many?" asked Orin.

"I don't know. It was less than twenty, but it was the entire patrol, I killed them all. I ain't proud of it. It was tragic to me. I was in Nam less than two days guys. I killed a few of them with my bare hands. I had to or they would have yelled out, but it was them or us."

"You know my brother they don't give out the Distinguished Service Cross for nothing. I personally think you should have got the Congressional Medal of Honor for that. I'll only say this once. It was an honor serving with you Peter and let's leave it at that," said Orin.

"I'll second that," added Nitro.

"I guess it's my turn to say FUCK YOU. You know how many times the four of you saved my life over there. The honor was mine. You guys are my heroes, and let's leave it at THAT."

The three guys laughed. The three women cried.

After that the proud women entered the room and sat next to their men.

Orin asked Peter, "Tell us Pete. How did you and Jennifer meet?"

"It was like this; Jennifer saw me walking down the street. She ran over and told me that I was the most handsome man she had ever seen and asked me if I would sleep with her. She sorts of begged so what could I say. I thought about it and finally said yes."

Not a slap in the arm but an actual punch in the arm followed.

"That is not true!!! Well, not all of it. He is kind of handsome. What happened was we met through a mutual friend of ours, Bob Stonemetz, he's the Mayor of Buffalo. Peter is on the board of directors of the Childrens Hospital there and I was joining the cause. Peter saw me and said I was the most beautiful woman he had ever seen and asked if I would sleep with him. I said, no way you are disgusting pig. So, he said well, then will you marry me, he sort of begged. So, what could I say, I said yes and the rest is history."

Nitro said, "That sounds a little more like it. Let's go with Jennifer's bullshit story instead of Peter's."

Everyone laughed and laughed.

"No, it's true we did meet at a charity thing. I was flat hooked. Will you look at this woman! She's even smarter than she is beautiful."

Nitro joked, "Well she can't be that damn smart. She's marrying you."

"That is so wrong on a multitude different levels," responded Peter.

"What does that mean exactly. Peter, how many times have I asked you not to use those big college words around me," he said smiling.

"Nitro, it means I am a very lucky man."

Betty and Sally said in unison, "Awwwww."

The rest of the night was nothing but a bunch of I love you man and the women bounding. It was perfect.

The next morning everyone was up early. The guys shared something else besides memories. Giant headaches. The girls had prepared a wonderful breakfast and forced their men to eat. It helped. After breakfast, Orin took everyone on a tour of Fort Bragg. They received a hero's welcome from almost everyone they met. Their reputations, even though it was a while ago, followed them. Peter had to admit it felt good.

The remainder of the weekend went great.

The wedding invitations and groomsmen requests were cemented, and Jennifer was fully accepted and totally established as one of them. It couldn't have gone any better.

The plan was for the four of them to come into town a little early so the guys could partake in the bachelor party.

Buffalo, New York will never be the same.

CONTI III
Change is Coming

Chapter 16

On their first day back in town Jennifer, Theresa and Colleen were busy putting together the invitations. Peter, Russell, and their dad were discussing the logistics of accommodations.

"I've got plenty of space here at my gigantic palace," said Peter.

"Why do you have to rub this place in my face. It's not a freekin palace. It just a mansion."

Both the brothers laughed.

"Grow up you two," snapped their father. "Get serious for once, will you boys? There are a lot of people coming in from out of town. You need a plan Peter."

"Dad, I have a plan, sort of," answered Peter. "As soon as we have the RSVP's and we have the number of out of town quests, I'll book a bank of rooms at the Ritz. I'll prepay for the rooms so people won't be put out expense wise. I can accommodate a bunch of people at my home, but I'm sure many of them would rather have the freedom to move around without moving all together in a herd. I know my army buddies would. They know they can stay at my place, but I think with everything going on before the wedding they'd probably rather have their own rooms. That's up to them."

"I have room at my home," injected Russell.

"Thanks bro, but not needed."

"I do have one set of guests that I absolutely need to stay with us, if they are able to come that is."

"Who's that son?"

"Dad, I plan on inviting my adopted family from Italy."

"I don't understand that relationship at all Peter. You barely know those people."

"Not true. Whatever you think you've heard about Vito Bansano has nothing to do with his brother Gino or any of his family. These people are wonderful, wonderful people. You've never come to grips with the relationship Vito and I had, and I'm not going to try and explain it again. Just realize the relationship was almost 20 years long. Vito in his heart adopted me without ever saying a word of that to me. BUT, to his family in the Old Country, he talked about me every time they spoke. When I brought his ashes there to his final resting place, I was accepted like a long-lost nephew. The warmth of these people was amazing. So much so that I call him Uncle Gino and I'm happy too. Just trust my judgment with this, please Dad.

"I have to admit, Vito Bansano must really have loved you son to have left you what he did. That is more than obvious."

"I'm glad you have at least come to that conclusion, but please, please don't put Gino in the same boat as Vito. They look identical but they are two completely different men. I don't know if they will come, but if I were a betting man, I bet they do. If they do, they will stay with me. I'll phone them myself with the invitation later today."

"Okay son, that's your decision and your life, but I don't get it."

"I do Pete. Glad to hear it. I'll keep an eye on them when they're here for you brother."

"Russ, I don't say it enough, but well you know."

"Me too Pete."

While the men were having their conversation, the women were working on invitations.

"I think we should put the diplomats all at one table," said Jennifer.

Colleen just smiled, "It is so crazy when you say that kind of stuff. It's hard for me to wrap my head around it."

"Coll, it was just a job. These people are my friends. Just think about it like that. Plus, not everyone will come. They're busy people."

"Theresa asked, "Alright, who are you sending invitations to."

"Well, Mr. And Mrs. George R. Fowler and."

"Wait, just wait one damn minute. You're inviting the President of the United States. Jesus Jenny," said a flustered Colleen.

"Yes Colleen, but they won't be able to attend. I have to invite them though, because Amanda will be mad at me if I don't at least send an invitation."

"Amanda Fowler, the First Lady," Colleen said shaking her head.

"Are you going to do this for everyone? I worked in Washington, D.C. Colleen. What can I say?"

"Sorry, Jennifer, it's just a lot to handle. Your weeks away from being my sister-in-law for crying out loud."

"Yes, isn't that great."

"Yes of course, but is it okay if I admire you?"

"For a little while, but that's it," Jenny said with a giant smile.

All three ladies laughed.

"I'll just jot down the names and we'll fill the addresses in later," said Jenny.
"Mayor Robert and Arlene Stonemetz of course----Senator James and Kim Tobias---
Chief of Staff Mark and Donna Stephens---and we better send one to Secretary of State Thomas Pearl. Mr Pearl won't come either, but I need to send the invitation just the same. I'd better send one to Senator Margaret and Dan Hixson. They won't attend, that's a formality only. That would be the dignitary table."

"WOW, WOW, WOW," said Colleen. "I had to say that."

They all laughed again.

"Theresa added, "OK, I have all the Millen's addresses here."

"Good," answered Jennifer. "Do we have the names and addresses of the people on the board at the Childrens Hospital?"

"I have them here Jenny," said Colleen.

"Excellent. Here's the list of the people from Washington, D.C., friends and co-workers," said Jenny as she handed the list to Theresa.

"Yes dear, I already have this list."

"What about my Uncle Frank and Aunt Patricia and the list of my friends and family in Rochester?"

"I have that list too and I have your Uncle and Aunt with me at our table," answered Theresa."

"That's perfect. Thank you, Mom. How about Father Jim Nahorski? Did we send out one to him? Peter already set it up with him, but I think we should send one out just the same."

"I have him right here," said Colleen.

"Let's not forget Hazel," added Jennifer.

"Got her too," said Colleen.

"I assume we have all of Peter's buddies' addresses. Sonny, Ray, Al, etc.," added Colleen.

"Of course, those pains will probably pick theres up. They're over here enough," said Jenny laughingly. "I'm starting to love them all. And I'll take care of the Green Beret friends as well.

Jenny continued with, "Well then. All that's left is that Peter wanted a few to hand out to a couple of his friends and he wanted to take care of the Bansano family in Italy. I think that's it," explained Jennifer.

"OH wait. I almost forgot, Antonio and Mary Scavazzo and their daughter Julie. I want them to understand they are not workers at the wedding. They're guests. We can just send those invitations to the restaurant," added Jenny.

Just as she said that, Peter walked in.

"I'm ready, let's get those invitations started.

"Is that a joke," said Theresa. "We're finished."

"Yes Mom. It was a joke. But I guess it wasn't funny."

"I thought it was extremely funny honey," said Jennifer.

"Are you just saying that to make me feel better?"

"Yes, what do you think?" replied Jenny sarcastically.

Everybody laughed.

"Well actually I did come in for a reason. I'm just getting ready to call Italy to invite the Bansanos so I wanted to grab an invitation to give them the details."

"Here you are son. You really have gotten close to that family, haven't you?"

"Yes Mom. I guess I have. Does that bother you at all?"

"Of course, not sweetheart. They sound like a very loving family and apparently, they have feeling for you. I hope they are able to come. I'm looking forward to meeting them."

"Thanks Mom. Jenny is completely wrong about you."

"WHAT!" said Jenny.

"We're even," laughed Peter, as he walked out of the room on his way to his office.

*   *   *

"Ciao," said Peter.

"Ciao," said Sofia, Uncle Gino's wife.

"E' Peter, Sofia. Calling from America."

"Hello Peter. How is you?" she replied.

"Molto bene, Sofia. Molto Bene. E tu?"

"Good. Everybody good."

"Bene," replied Peter

"Is Uncle Gino there?"

"Uno momento Peter."

Gino was excited when Sofia told him who was on the phone. "Peter, I am very happy you called. How are you?" asked Gino Bansano.

"I'm good. How are you Uncle Gino? "Are you feeling any better? The loss of your friend Paulo took a toll on you. I'm so sorry."

"Yes, Peter, but life goes on."

"Is something wrong. Why are you calling?"

"The opposite. I'm calling you to ask if you would come to America the end of May. Uncle Gino, I'm getting married."

"Fantastico. That is wonderful news my American nephew."

"Just get here Uncle Gino and I will take care of everything once you're here. You will stay with me and Jennifer and we'll pick you up at the airport when you land. Do you think you can make it? I know it's a long way, but I would love if you could come."

"Uno momento Peter. Sofia?" Gino was back on the phone within in seconds. "Yes Peter, we will be there. Thank you for asking us."

"Uncle Gino, I would buy your airline tickets, but I would need your passports. I will definitely reimburse you when you get here."

"Don't be silly my boy. This is an honor for us. I am very happy for you. Tell me about your almost wife."

"She is beautiful like a sunset. She is a smart, loving, caring, accomplished woman. I am blessed Uncle Gino. Blessed.

"This news is fantastico. I cannot wait to meet her and your family. What day you want us to come?"

"The wedding is June 1 but come before and I will show you our city and you can spend some time with my mother and father and my brother Russell. They are all anxious to meet you. Come whenever you want. You are welcome in my home as long as you would like. Angelina and Alberto are invited as well. I have plenty of room."

"Molto bene. Molto bene. I am very happy for you. Very happy for you, but we can stay in a hotel. I do not want to put you out."

"Ha ha ha, that is funny. NO. My house is your house. I won't take no for an answer. I have a very large home. We will not even know you are there."

"OK, I can see I waste my breath. I will call now and make reservations and call you back. Also, I will inform Angelina and let you know if she can make it, but count on Sofia and me to be there. Thank you, Peter, for thinking of us."

"Uncle Gino, you are part of my family now, and never out of my mind."

CONTI III
Change is Coming

Chapter 17

The wedding day was growing near. Jennifer and her friends had a wonderful bachlorette party thrown by Gwen and the girls. It wasn't totally crazy, but it definitely got druck out for a few of them. Frankie Ann threw up in the limo. The boy's party was coming up on Friday. Orin and Nitro were coming in on Thursday night with their wives. Betty and Sally were all set to bail their husbands out of jail. When are these guys going to grow up?

It was Tuesday morning and the Bansano's plane was arriving from Italy at noon. Peter and Jennifer were waiting at the International Gate for them.

"I hope they like me," said Jenny.

"Are you kidding? They will love you. I'm the one who's a little nervous. You know my dad and everything."

"You shouldn't be sweetheart. Your father is a wonderful man. I guarantee you he'll behave."

"I hope so. Oh, there they are. Uncle Gino, Sofia, over here."

The Bansanos walked over to where the couple was standing and the first words out of both their mouths simultaneously were, " E Molto Bella (She is very beautiful)."

"Mille Grazie," said Jennifer to everyone's surprise.

Peter made the introductions. They all hugged.

Sofia asked Jennifer, "Parli Italiano?"

Jennifer answered, "Solo un po. (Just a little.)"

Sofia smiled and said, "I speak English very bad, but a little too."

Gino then said, "I speak English pretty okay so let me say, Sofia and I would like to thank you for inviting us to your wedding. It makes us very happy that Peter has found such an intelligent, beautiful woman."

"Thank you, Mr. Bansano."

"Please call me Uncle Gino. Peter does."

"I can tell you; Peter speaks very highly of both of you. I have been anxiously waiting to meet you. I can see why he feels the way he does. He's right, you are wonderful people."

"Milli Grazzi," said Sofia.

"I see you've already been through customs so let's load up your bags and take a little tour of our city," said Peter.

Sofia asked, "Can we see the Niagara Falls?"

Peter smiled and said, "Of course Sofia. We'll go there for lunch. Later we will have dinner at my parent's home. They are also anxious to meet you."

"Fantastico," said Gino.

It was a perfect afternoon. They ate at the Niagara Tower Restaurant overlooking the Falls. The look on Sofia's face when she first saw the Falls was priceless. Gino acted like it wasn't all that much, but deep inside he was every bit as excited.

They left the restaurant and headed to Peter's home to drop off their luggage and freshen up first, before going to Peter's childhood home.

You could hear a gasp as they pulled up the circle drive to the entrance of Peter and Jennifer's home.

Peter said, "Uncle Gino, this is how successful your brother Vito was in this country. This is Vito's home."

"No Peter. This is your home. My brother wanted you to have this. He had said that to me many times. Many times. Never forget that."

"Come in. Please. Come in," said Jennifer.

Peter added, "Make yourselves at home. Let me show you to your room."

Sofia walked in and immediately said, "Molto Bella."

Hazel was there to greet them and asked if they would like anything.

Peter answered, "Mr. and Mrs. Bansano, this is Hazel. She is like one of the family. She is simply great."

Gino answered, "Nice to meet you. Nothing now my dear, but maybe later."

"Anything you want any time you want it Mr. and Mrs. Bansano. I worked for you brother sir. He was a wonderful man."

"Millie Grazzi," answered Sofia.

"Thank you very much Miss Hazel. Very nice of you to say," answered Gino.

They all went to their rooms to freshen up and get ready to go to meet Peter's folks.

There was mystique in the air as Peter and Jennifer brought their Italian guests into the Conti house. Peter had no idea how his father would react to Gino and Sofia Bansano.

Theresa was her warm self as she greeted them at the door.

"Mr. and Mrs. Bansano, Peter has mentioned you so many times I feel like I already know you. Please come in. I'm Theresa, Peter's mom. What a pleasure to finally meet you."

"Grazzi, Mrs. Conti. I am Gino and this is my wife Sofia. I could not wait to meet the wonderful woman and man who raised such a man as Peter. Your son has brought joy into our lives when there was sadness. Peter made the passing of my brother Vito feel like he wasn't gone at all. I'm sure Peter has told you how my brother felt about your son. Now Sofia and I, and my family back home, feel the same way about him. What a great job you and your husband have done raising such a man."

"Oh, my, what a wonderful thing to say. Welcome to our home."

With that Thomas walked up next to his wife. Peter held his breath as his father spoke.

Thomas, after hearing what Gino Bansano just said, held out his hand and replied, "Gino, I'm Thomas. You honor Theresa and me with your words. Peter has told us what warm and caring people you are, and you just showed how true his words were. Gino, Sofia, welcome to America, welcome to our home, and welcome to our family."

Everyone hugged. To Peter it was perfect.

Russell, Colleen, and Maria, who came in from her home in Lockport, just outside of the greater Buffalo area, were next to greet the Bansanos.

Russell stuck out his hand to shake Gino's and said, "Felice di conoscerti (happy to meet you). Did I say that right? I'm Russell, Peter's brother, and this is my wife Colleen. This young lady is our sister Maria."

Gino shook Russell's hand, but Sofia just answered, "Si, yes, Russell, you say right. Mille Grazzi."

Russ just smiled and said, "That's all the Italian I know, and I had to memorize that."

Everyone laughed.

"Siediti (have a seat)," said Thomas. "Theresa and I both were raised in Italian homes and know some Italian but to carry on a conversation would be difficult. Do you want us to try or do you speak English better than our Italian?"

Gino replied, "Thomas. Is alright I call you Thomas? I have learned your language over the years. I have a Ristorante in Sorrento and have many American guests, so I learn. Sofia knows enough. English would be fine, no problem."

"Bene. Good, Peter has told us you have adopted our son into your family. For that I will say thank you. It has made our son happy. So forever it will be first names. Agreed?"

"Yes, Mille Grazzi. You make Sofia and me feel very welcome."

Theresa spoke next, "I have always been told that my Italian cooking is very good. Now I am nervous to have experts try it. If you do not like it, I am willing to listen and learn."

"If your mama teaches you, you have learned all you need I think," answered Sofia. "I think you worry for no reason. Gino think he is best cook ever, but now we will see, huh Gino."

"Why you say this when you know it is true, I am best cook in world."

Everyone laughed.

They sat down to a fantastic meal served by Theresa. She worked all afternoon preparing it and when the meal was through Gino Bansano said, "Theresa, now I am second best cook in world."

Everyone laughed again.

Thomas, Gino, Peter, and Russell sat in the living room drinking Irish coffee while the women sat in the kitchen drinking coffee without the whiskey in it. The conversations in both rooms were comfortable to all. Gino talked about Peter. Gino, knowing so much about Peter from conversations with Vito, made everyone at ease. The only moment that Peter actually held his breath was when he was waiting for his father's response when he called Gino, Uncle Gino. He called him that when he asked him if he wanted more coffee. Thomas didn't flinch at all. He understood why Peter felt that way about the man. Gino felt like family to Thomas as well.

The night was perfect.

Peter invited his father and Gino to go with them Friday night for the bachelor party. The two older gentlemen agreed that they would have a drink with everyone at Peter's where everyone was meeting but would not be going when they left. Again perfect.

"Gino, when the boys leave for their party, Theresa and I would like to show you and your lovely wife Sofia more of our town. If you would like to stay with us that night or, for that matter, the whole time, you are more than welcome."

"Thank you, Thomas. We are already settled in at Peter's home, but Sofia and I would like to spend much time with you and Theresa. That would be very nice. Very nice."

"Great. At the wedding you will sit with us at our table."

"Mille Grazzi. You make my wife and I feel very welcome."

"Well, you are family."

Everyone, especially Peter, smiled.

CONTI III
Change is Coming

Chapter 18

Peter and Jenny were at the airport again on Thursday morning. This time they were waiting for the Green Beret crowd. They actually made a scene when they all got together. The thing is these guys just didn't care. Betty, Sally, and Jenny just watched their men make fools out of themselves and were happy to watch. These men were close.

"Ladies, here's the deal," Peter said to Betty and Sally. "We will definitely be going to the house and I told you it's a pretty big house, didn't I? It has way too many bedrooms for just Jenny and me, so I hope you all chose to stay with us there. You don't have to decide now, BUT just in case I do have a bank of reservations at the Ritz Carlton if you decide you would like to have a little more privacy. Totally up to you gals because these fools would sleep in a car if they had to."

"I'm not rushing your decision, but PLEASE stay with us. I'm just saying," said Jenny.

Nitro spoke up and said, "Let's see this freekin mansion you keep telling us about. You been bragging about it like a little schoolboy for Christ's sakes."

"I have not," answered Peter.

"BOYS!" said Sally looking directly at Nigel when she said it.

"I want to see the place myself Peter," said Orin. "I'm still wheeling from the comment you made a few months back when you casually said, by the way, I'm rich."

"Okay, maybe I exaggerated a little, but the house is nice," said Peter smiling at Jenny. She smiled a knowing smile back at him.

When they pulled up, you could hear a pin drop in the car. They got out and Nitro was the first to speak, "You have got to be kidding me. What the fuck!!"

"Well maybe I didn't exaggerate."

Orin looked at his wife and said, "Betty?"

"OH YEAH, we're staying here."

"HELL YES," said Sally with her mouth wide open.

"Peter, really man, how?" asked Orin.

"Inherited, don't get your panties in a bunch," he said. "Come on in. You haven't seen anything yet."

Peter gave them the full tour and people who don't get impressed very often were impressed. It's not like they're paupers. They are all successful people, but this place truly is impressive.

Jenny suggested, "There is a guest quarters back by the pool that has two bedrooms, a kitchenette, and a sitting room if you would like to stay there instead of the big house."

"Well that's about perfect," answered Betty. "Peter, Jenny, we are so happy for you guys. My God. In fact, God has definitely blessed you."

"Thank you, Betty. You never know what life has in store for you, do you?"

Nitro then said, "Peter, I have a question."

"Shoot."

"Can you lend me some money?"

"Are you serious?" asked Peter.

"Go fuck yourself," responded Nitro.

"That was uncalled for Nitro," interjected Orin. "But I have to admit I was thinking about asking for a loan myself."

Everyone laughed. Peter wasn't trying to brag. Not in the least, but he was happy they decided to stay with them. It made the whole wedding experience that much better.

Minutes later Peter's folks walked in. The entire grouped hugged. Thomas asked Orin about his parents. They had met them a number of times and the Contis consider the Olsons like family.

"What's up Mom?" asked Jenny.

"Nothing, we just wanted to greet the boys and their wives for one thing and we're picking up the Bansanos to go to lunch."

"Oh God. I forgot about Uncle Gino for a minute. These guys make me crazy Ma. Will you ask them to leave please? They're already bothering me."

Peter got the usual slap in the arm from his mother.

"We're grabbing the Bansanos. We knew us old people would be in the way. You kids go have a good time," said Thomas.

Kids. He called a Green Beret Colonel and Major, kids, but to him they were just his son's friends.

Gino and Sofia came out of their room and greeted the Contis and Peter's friends. The introductions went well. Peter explained who the

Bansanos were to his friends and who the soldiers were to the Bansanos and at the same time gave them all a little insight on each other.

The older crowd took off and left the youngsters to do what they were planning on doing in the first place.

Jenny asked Betty and Sally if they had any particular place they wanted to see first. The two women answered in unison, "Niagara Falls."

Peter took them for lunch at the same place he took the Bansanos, the Tower Restaurant. Niagara Falls is without doubt the first-place newcomers to the Buffalo/ Niagara Falls area want to see. As a matter of fact, it really doesn't matter how many times people see the spectacle, it never ceases to amaze. It's simply spectacular.

After a great lunch, they headed back to Peter's for some adult refreshments and a little R and R around the pool. Jenny was taking the girls out that evening for a nice dinner and the men were meeting the crew to party until the cows come home. It was going to be a fun night to say the least.

Sonny, Ray, and Al were the first to show. They had met Peter's army buddies before and, as always, had nothing but respect for the guys. Who wouldn't? Russell came soon after accompanied by Peter's brother-in-law Tommy, Peter's father-in-law Mike, and Thomas and Gino. A few of Jennifer's friend's husbands, that Peter had become friends with came next; Joe, his brother Steve, Kurt, and Rafael. They sat around and drank at Peter's for a while. Those who hadn't seen the place were impressed. That's an understatement. The bus showed up around 7:30 p.m. equipped with a fully stocked bar. It was going to get mighty drunk out that's a given.

Thomas, Mike and Gino said their goodbyes and wished them a safe night. Thomas yelled at his sons to behave. All the guys laughed.

It was started.

First stop was the casino at the Indian Reservation just outside of town in Silvercreek. The men dismounted the bus with the plan to meet back there at 10:00 p.m. That didn't really need to be said because they all stuck together while they were there anyway.

The group was at the crowded bar making a plan when the crowd parted, and three gentlemen passed through the opening the people made like they were royalty.

"Peter Conti. Hey Peter," said Tony Sotto.

"Tony. Hello," responded Peter.

We can't stay buddy and unfortunately, I won't be able to make the wedding on Sunday. The fact that you sent the invitation was a very nice thing and appreciated, you know what I mean," said Sotto with his hand held out to shake Peter's.

"How did you know we were here Tony?" asked Peter.

"You don't think I hear things?" answered Tony.

"I'm glad you're here. Hello Joe, Vic. Too many of us for introductions so I'll just say, guys, these are former business partners of mine. Tony, Joe, Vic, the guys." "Can you guys stay? Join us."

"Would love to Peter, but we can't. You know, business. Just wanted to congratulate you on your upcoming wedding. Nice to meet you all! You've got a good man and a good friend here guys. Drink up everyone, the drinks are all on me. Have a good night."

The three of them shook Peter's hand and they were gone as soon as they came.

"What the hell," said Nitro.

"They're friends from a previous life is all I can say."

Tommy Kline, Peter's brother-in-law, asked, "Was that Anthony Sotto?"

Peter simply answered, "Yes."

There were a few whispers amongst them, but nothing revealing. Just that they were well known men with somewhat dangerous reputations. Peter brushed it off and the party continued.

Russell was winning pretty big and getting a little rowdy at the crap table when one of the tougher looking patrons walked over to him.

The guy got very close to Russ and said something the other guys didn't hear. Nitro was the closest to Russ when the guy leaned on Russ a little too zealously. Peter was moving towards the scene at a pretty rapid pace but didn't get there before Nitro.

"Lay a finger on him pal and I'll break every fucking bone in your body," said Nitro angrily.

"Who the fuck are you?" said the stranger in a verboten tone.

Nitro smiled and said, "Nitro Burke, Special Forces Green Beret. Who the fuck are you?"

"Someone who's leaving right this minute."

"Nice to meet you someone. Bye."

Russell turned to Nitro and said, "I could have handled that Nitro."

"I know Russ. I just like to show off."

Everybody laughed, but the guys at the party who didn't know Nitro or Orin truly realized who they were.

They hit a number of bars on their journey to drunkville and ended up at Peter's. It was inevitable that the conversation at some time would get around to the three Green Berets and Vietnam.

"I can tell you all about Nam in a few words," said Nitro. "It sucked."

"I was there," said Al. "And I second that shit."

The Rochester boys and Tommy were all ears waiting to hear about some of the heroics, but these guys seldom talk about that stuff.

Tommy questioned Peter though.

"Tommy, all I can tell you is it was fucking hot, the hookers were diseased, the beer was warm, and the food sucked. Other than that, it was nice," answered Peter.

Orin said, "I'll tell you something about the future groom here though. Man, could this guy shoot."

"Yeah," said Nitro. "When Peter joined the unit, Orin was a Captain, and he told me, Joe LaVaca, and Tom (WilliamTell) Tully what he heard about our buddy Peter here. He was told Peter could shoot the dick off a hummingbird from a hundred yards. You know what, whoever said that was right."

"Fuck you guys. You all could shoot every bit as good as me. You just stuck me with that job cause you didn't like to climb trees."

Russell asked, "You were a sniper?"

Peter felt like he had to answer, after all, it was his brother who asked. "Yes, but my team, including these two assholes, could all shoot."

"How many gooks did you guys kill over there?" asked a drunken Sonny.

"Enough my friend. It was war," answered Orin. "That's enough of that bullshit talk."

"I know what we can kill," said Nitro. "This bottle of Crown Royal. Who's up for that?"

141

The conversation turned into talk about kids and jobs and everything you could think of. But one thing resonated in all these guys. Peter, Orin, and Nitro were some badass motherfuckers and there was no denying that. Special Forces Green Beret, it doesn't get much tougher than that.

They drank almost through the night. Peter had plenty of beds for every one of the guys who were able to get to a bed, there was no way any of them could drive.

They were all going to pay the price in the morning.

CONTI III
Change is Coming

Chapter 19

It's Saturday morning and the drunks were starting to move around. Hazel had a variety of Danish pastries, coffee cakes, bagels, muffins, and toast laid out with a vast amount of coffee available for the taking. The aspirin bottle was on the table as well. Most of the guys were sitting around the table head in hand and complaining.

"Never again," said Russell as he sipped his coffee.

Jennifer, Betty, and Sally were helping Hazel dole out the breakfast. Jenny turned to Russell and said, "Don't come crying to me. Nobody forced you to drink that much.

"Sis, would it be asking too much to ask you to just kill me."

"It looks like you guys were trying to do a good job of that yourselves."

Peter, Orin, and Nitro entered the breakfast room just about the same time.

Orin said as he walked in, "Would someone please answer the phone?"

His wife Betty responded with, "The phone is not ringing."

Orin then said, "OH my head."

The guys tried to laugh, but they couldn't.

"Hi honey," said Nitro.

"Don't you honey, me. Do you know how drunk you were last night?"

"I know I drank a little more than I should have."

"You peed the bed."

"I DID?"

"No, but that's how drunk you were that you don't even know."

This time the guys did laugh.

"Don't you dare laugh Mr. Conti," said Jennifer.

"They made me drink; I swear sweetheart. I LOVE YOU." was his response.

Jenny then looked at her friend Joe, Gwen's husband, and said, "And you Joe, were you laying on the floor all night? Disgusting."

"I guess I got drunk."

The guys laughed again.

The girls were not mad at all. They were just having a little fun with the guys. To them it was sort of cute.

After a while, the crew started heading back to their homes. Not much was said. Sonny, Ray, and Al all left together. Russ and Tommy were right behind them. The Rochester boys were getting to go cups for the drive back. It's about a two-hour drive. The army buddies were just kicking back.

The women were meeting with Theresa, Colleen, and Marie to go to the get their nails and hair done. Jennifer took Sofia with them. The guys just laid around like bums. Gino was spending the day with Thomas.

Peter and Orin were feeling a lot better by midday. Nitro was still eating aspirin like they were M&M's.

Out of nowhere Orin asked Peter, "Who were those guys we met at the Casino?"

"People who were in my life during all the Russian mob stuff. Does that sort of clear it up for you?"

"Enough said. But someday I'd like to hear the whole story."

"Someday buddy. It's better you don't know, and I'll leave it at that."

Sofia was having the time of her life. Theresa and Jennifer treated her like long lost family and Sofia returned the feelings in kind. It was a very nice day for the women to say the least. Thomas and Gino spent the day just bonding. Thomas truly understood why Peter felt the way he did about these people. Peter was right; they are warm, caring, wonderful people. Originally Thomas was mad at Peter, when Peter told the family he bought a villa over there, but never said anything. Thomas thought it was impulsive and a waste of money. Now he's looking forward to seeing it. Gino had invited the Contis to visit them in Italy numerous times over the course of the week. Thomas was definitely going to take them up on their offer at some time in the future. They had grown to be friends.

Saturday blew by like it was but hours long. Peter and Jenny hosted a nice dinner at the house for friends and family. There is a BBQ restaurant in Buffalo, Woody's BBQ, that brings a giant BBQ grill on site and supplies not just the BBQ but all the fixings as well. Perfect, everyone enjoyed it. Especially Hazel, who was invited just like she was family.

Sunday was but a night sleep away and Jennifer was thrilled to the bone. It was her wedding day.

CONTI III
Change is Coming

Chapter 20

Jennifer Taylor Grier looked so beautiful in her wedding dress that the people there were actually gawking. Peter himself was speechless. Sonny, who is usually so quick with a line, didn't say a word. He just patted Peter on the back.

Colonel Olson and Major Burke ushered the family and friends to their seats. Orin escorted the Contis to the groom's side and Nitro walked Patricia Taylor to the brides. Her husband Frank was walking his niece down the aisle.

Father Nahorski was wonderful performing the ceremony. Peter wished he could comprehend what his friend the priest was saying. He just couldn't concentrate because he couldn't take his eyes off of Jennifer. To say she looked radiant would not due her justice.

When Father Jim said you may now kiss the bride, the kiss that followed was almost embarrassing. Peter DID NOT CARE.

Many people were crying for various reasons, but all out of happiness.

The newlyweds walked down the aisle both smiling like they won the lottery. Each of them felt like they just did. This was a perfect marriage for two deserving people.

The entourage headed to Antonio's for the reception.

The place looked magnificent. Antonio and family outdid themselves. As soon as Peter and Jenny walked in, and I mean seconds, Peter was looking for Antonio.

"My friend, I don't know what to say. Your place looks absolutely wonderful. I have no words to thank you."

Antonio smiled and answered, "Peter, I hear you my friend and I thank you for the compliment, but the thanks comes from me. I don't know what I would have done if you wouldn't have stepped into our situation. You have no idea, but I think I would have killed that man. Prison means nothing to me when it comes to my Julie. I can never repay you."

"Antonio, there is no debt. That is just what friends do."

"Yes Peter. And this is what I do when that friend gets married."

"Thank you, Antonio."

"NO, Thank you Peter."

That's all Peter could do at the moment, but there was no way he would allow Antonio to lose business, spend the kind of money he must have spent to decorate and change the seating, and pay for the food. That couldn't be. Peter realized if he tried in any way to give Antonio money it would insult the man to his core. He just tucked away in his mind this thought, "When Julie gets married, she won't believe how much money there would be as a gift in her wedding card." That's a given.

The ambiance was superb. The small four-piece ensemble was perfect, and just too good to be called a band. The food was phenomenal, and the people melded together like they knew each other for years.

Sonny tapped his glass to quiet the crowd for the Best Man's speech. He stood up and raised his glass and said, "I've known Roger almost my entire life."

Ray whispered something as planned.

"I mean Peter."

Everyone laughed.

"It's impossible to have a better friend. He's the brother I never had."

Al whispered something as planned.

"Oh, that's right, I do have a brother. Well, anyway, I know this is one of the happiest days in Peter's life, second only to meeting me. So, with that said he joked, HERE'S TO ME."

Everyone laughed and laughed.

He continued with, "No seriously. What a joyous day for all of us and especially for my best friend and his new absolutely, and I'm not kidding, this is not an exaggeration, beautiful wife Jennifer. As a matter of fact, how about a round of applause for how beautiful Jennifer looks in her wedding gown."

The entire place erupted in applause.

"There you go Jenny. Did I earn my money?"

Everyone laughed again.
He finished by saying, "To the newlyweds, Peter and Jennifer, I wish you long life and happiness forever. Salute!"

Sonny sat down to a rousing round of applause, and then Peter got up.

"Sonny, thank you my friend, for a lifetime of friendship. As a matter of fact, I want to thank everyone sitting here at the wedding table for their deep friendships as well. I have no words that could explain what you all mean to Jennifer and me. We are simply lucky people to have you in our lives. Jennifer and I would like to take this time to thank every one of you for coming. I should actually name each of you by name because you are that close to us, but that would take too long. Just know we love you all. This is not a speech like they do at the Academy Awards where you thank everyone you've ever known, but there are a few people I have to single out. My Mother and Father for, simply, everything there is in my life. To Jennifer's and now my new Uncle Frank and Aunt Patricia. Jenny just wanted to make sure I told you how much she loves you. To my brother, his wife, and my sister. I don't need to say anything because they know how I feel. I want to say a special thank you to all you folks who traveled from Washington, D.C. to be with Jennifer on this special day, especially Senator Tobias and his wife Kim and Mark Stephens, the honorable Chief of Staff to the President, and his lovely wife Donna. Jennifer and I say thank you all for coming. Thank you to our industrious mayor, Robert Stonemetz and his awesome wife Arlene. If I didn't say his name, he'd be mad for months so there you go, your honor. Well, to be fair, he did introduce Jenny and me to one another so let me rephrase that. Thank you very much Bob. Very much! I guess I had more thank yous than I thought because I need to thank the people who traveled the farthest, all the way from Sorrento, Italy; my adopted Aunt and Uncle, Gino and Sofia Bansano. Thank you for being here, it means a lot to me. All of you in this room are family to me. I see my other family is here to celebrate with us. Thank you to the Millen family. I know Jenny and I are saying a lot of thank yous, but they are all truly heart felt. The guys who look like they just got off a troop train, let me tell you, don't mess with them because there is definitely something wrong with them, they're crazy. But just the same, thank you and yours my good friends and comrades for being here and for your service to our country. And last, but not least, our hosts of this magnificent dinner and fabulous party Antonio and Mary Scavazzo. Antonio, I have no words. Thank you, my friend. Spectacular. And to all of you from Jennifer and me, thank you for being here on our special day. Now just enjoy the rest of the evening. I need to sit down next to my wife now. I love saying those words, my wife.

Cheers came from all. The music started and Jennifer and Peter had their first dance as husband and wife. The wedding party joined in.

The rest of the night was perfect. Jennifer was so happy that two or three times during the night she just teared up. It was the happiest day of her life.

If there was such a thing as a perfect wedding, it just happened.

CONTI III
Change is Coming

Chapter 21

Seeing as they had a house full of company, Peter and Jenny decided to delay their honeymoon until all were gone. Monday morning found Peter's Army buddies and their wives sitting around and drinking coffee out at the pool.

Orin looked up to see Jenny coming out of the breakfast room door carrying a tray of pastries.

"What in the world are you doing girl? You should be on your honeymoon," said Orin.

"Don't be silly. We have the rest of our lives to do that, but you all will only be here a short time, so Peter and I want to spend time with you."

"Then we'll leave today."

Peter walked out right behind his new wife and said, "Absolutely not. We have the Bansanos here too. You said your flights were leaving Wednesday and Uncle Gino's is Wednesday as well. We'll go after that. When the smoke clears, Jenny and I are going to take a nice long trip to Europe and end up at our villa in Italy."

Nitro spit out his coffee when Peter said that and said, "Your villa in Italy. What the frigg. Jesus Peter."

"I told you Nitro, inheritance. What can I say?"

"How about saying would you guys like to join us at our villa in Italy?"

"Okay, how would you guys like to join us at our villa in Italy?"

"No thanks, how about another time?"

Everybody laughed.

"Anytime," said Jenny.

The four friends lifted their coffee cups in acknowledgement.

"Good," said Peter. "We'll set that up because we plan on staying there for a while. Why rush back here."

"I want your life," said Orin.

Everyone laughed again.

Gino Bansano stuck his head out of the door and asked, "Is Okay if we join your young people?"

Almost in unison they said, "Of course. Come on out."

The Bansano's came out holding a cup of coffee that Hazel had poured for them and sat. They were all smiles as they got the chance to really talk to Peter's friends.

"You are the men that fought together with Peter I was told."

"Yes Sir," answered Orin.

"My brother, God rest his soul, spoke of all of you. I am proud to know you as your accomplishments were many. You are brave men."

"Thank you, Sir. We were just doing our jobs," answered Orin.

"That's what heroes say," replied Gino.

"I like him," injected Nitro.

Everyone laughed once more.

Peter then changed the subject and asked, "The horses are running at Fort Erie over in Canada today. Is everyone up for the races?"

"Hell yes," said Orin. He stopped for a second and looked at Betty. She shook her head up and down. "Hell yes," said Orin again.

Everyone laughed again.

"Yeah, I'm tough alright," added Orin.

The laughing continued.

"Peter, we told your parents we would have lunch with them today," said Gino.

"I'll call them. We can all go if you'd like."

"That would be nice," answered Sofia.

Peter made the call and three hours later they were all standing next to the finish line at Erie Downs Racetrack. Peter was teaching those who didn't know how to read a racing form, the idiosyncrasies of it. Bets were flying. The women pooled their money and ended up winning more than they were losing. It wasn't about money at all with the guys. It was all about bragging rights. Thomas and Gino teamed up too and ended up $30 ahead and stuck it to the young boys. It was perfect. They left the track and, since they were already in Canada, the consensus amongst all the out-of-towners was to go back to the Tower Restaurant for lunch.

That was a perfect idea. It doesn't matter how many times you see the awesomeness of the water flowing over the falls, it's always a magnificent sight.

It was a great lunch. Everyone had a wonderful time. The only trouble came when the check was brought. It almost turned into a scene. Then it ended when Gino spoke, "I would like to ask you all if you would please allow me to pay. The hospitality shown Sofia and me by Peter and Jennifer, not to mention Thomas and Theresa, has been so outstanding that this very small gesture is all we have to say thank you. Please."

Thomas answered for everyone, "NO."

Then Theresa stepped in, "Thank you Gino and Sofia. It is not necessary, but of course."

Orin then said, "What are we bologna? Don't we have a say?"

Betty then said, "ORIN."

Everyone at the table said in unison, "Thank you Gino and Sofia." And that was that.

They ate most of their meals out until flight time, so Orin and Nitro did not allow another bill to be paid by anyone but them. They can be quite convincing. Thomas tried, but Peter let him know how futile his efforts actually were.

Wednesday came and the festivities were over. The Green Beret group left with tears shed by Jennifer. She got very close to Betty and Sally and the guys too for that matter.

Thomas and Theresa went to the airport with Peter and Jennifer to wish the Bansanos bon voyage. Gino and Sofia were adamant about Thomas and Theresa visiting them in Sorrento and it didn't take all that much convincing for the Contis to accept. Peter informed everyone right there at the airport that Jenny and he were planning on spending some time traveling through Europe for their honeymoon and that they planned on ending up in Sorrento. He told them all they had planned on staying in Italy for an extended period of time. The Bansanos were thrilled. The Contis were not.

"How long is an extended period of time?" asked Theresa.

"I really don't know Ma. I haven't even stayed in my new place, I mean our place, yet and all I can tell you is that the entire area is paradise. The place is situated on the side of the cliffs that overlook the Mediterranean Sea. It takes your breath away just looking out at it. Everything about the place says stay a while. So, I guess I'll leave it up to Jennifer. It will be at least 6 months though."

"Six months. That's too long son," said Thomas.

"Dad just come and visit. You won't want to leave. Believe me."

Gino stepped into the conversation by saying, "Thomas, come. Our home is your home."

Theresa answered, "Thank you Gino and Sofia. We will come to visit, but don't put us on the spot to say we will stay with you only because our son has a home there too."

"Understand Theresa," said Sofia. "Just know you are welcome."

The group hugged and kissed one another and off went the Bansanos.

Thomas turned to his son as they started to leave the airport and said, "Son, those were two of the nicest people I have ever met in my life. Please forgive me for doubting you. As far as your mother and I are concerned, the man IS your uncle."

"Just come to the Amalfi Coast folks. As soon as we're settled in, bring Russ, Colleen, and Maria too if they want. Trust me our place can accommodate all of you. It's pretty nice."

Thomas answered, "I'll bet it is son. I'll bet it is."

CONTI III
Change is Coming

Chapter 22

Three weeks later Jenny and Peter were looking out upon the City of Lights. That was their view from their perch at the top of the Eiffel Tower, 1000 feet above the magnificent city of Paris, France. It was breathtaking.

"Well Mrs. Conti, your wish is my command."

"Thank you honey. I've always dreamt of standing right here on this very spot with the man of my dreams. And right now, both of those things have come true."

"Sweetheart, the beauty I'm looking at is not this city. It's you."

"Peter, you have got the best lines. I swear."

"That wasn't a line."

"Peter?"

"Jennifer, is it alright if I think my wife is beautiful?"

"I'm sorry, I just figured you said that because you were horney."

"Well, that too."

They both laughed.

Paris was every bit as romantic as Jennifer had hoped. What a start of what was going to be a fabulous honeymoon.

The next day found them standing under the Arc de Triomphe, right after finishing a very nice breakfast of coffee and croissants, that is. The afternoon was spent at the Louvre Museum. Jenny loved every second of it. She was in heaven, and Peter loved Jenny so much, he liked it too. They went back to the room at the hotel afterwards for a nap. There was no sleeping. After a lovely dinner they took a walk and ended up at a beautiful park on the Champ de Mars, the street the Eiffel Tower was on, just to admire the Tower again. After some pleasant conversation, they got up from the bench they were sitting on to leave. All of a sudden three shady looking guys approached them.

"Stand behind me," said Peter to his wife.

The man who was probably the leader of the others walked up to Peter and asked, "Do you have a light?"

"No, I don't smoke," answered Peter.

The man pulled out a knife and said, "Then just give us your money."

The other two guys stood next to their leader right in front of Peter. They were all holding knives. Peter started to reach for his wallet. It's only money and he wasn't going to risk Jennifer in any way over a few hundred dollars.

"OK, just leave us alone."

Then the head guy made a bad mistake. He reached for Jenny's arm and said, "Take off that ring you're wearing and give it to me."

Peter's foot came up immediately, karate style, and caught the robber square under his jaw, knocking him out instantly. He dropped like a rock. Peter's next move was to kick the next guy's wrist that held the knife he was holding, and the knife went flying. At the same time Peter stretched out his four fingers like a weapon and shoved them into that guy's throat. He went down clutching his throat and was gasping for air. That left the third guy who was trying to slash at Peter with his knife.

"Your two friends will live, but, if you don't turn and run right now, I'll kill you where you stand."

The young man turned and was gone in seconds.

"Oh, dear God Peter. Are you alright?"

"Ask those imbeciles not me," he said. "I would have given them the money but when that ass-hole reached for you, I lost it, sorry honey. The question is are you alright?"

"What are we going to do? That one fella looks like he's dying."

"They'll be alright. Let's just leave. I've got an idea, how does a nice espresso sound to you?"

"Peter, who are you, really?"

"I don't know how I get myself in these situations. I have no luck. Until I met you that is."

"Why do you have to make light of everything? Those guys had knives,"

"And now they don't. Let it go. It's over."

"My God Peter. You amaze me."

"Sweetheart, compared to what I've had to deal with in my life, that wasn't much. Let this go. Don't let this incident spoil anything. You're safe with me."

"That's for sure. Have I told you lately that I love you?"

"Why, yes you have. Just this afternoon as a matter of fact."

They both laughed, but Jennifer was well aware of the man she married. Yes, Peter was charming, handsome, and debonair, but he was also a very dangerous man. Not in a scary way, just a very dangerous man.

They left Paris the next morning. Next stop, London.

They saw everything on their list in London. Big Ben, London's iconic timepiece, the Tower of London, the magnificent castle that houses the Crown Jewels, Buckingham Palace, the home of the Queen, and the Tower Bridge, the suspension bridge built in 1894 that crosses the famous River Thames. England was great.

"Where to next Mrs. Conti?"

"Barcelona, here we come," answered Jennifer.

They were flying by the seat of their pants. No agenda. Life was good for the Contis.

Barcelona was majestic. They stayed in the charming Gothic Quarters. A quaint area with narrow medieval streets lined with trendy bars, clubs, and Catalan restaurants. Everywhere you looked you would find vendors selling all kinds of things, leather, jewelry, and flowers galore. There were also all kinds of local foods available too. While they were there, they toured the famous Picasso Museum, then La Rambla. La Rambla is a tree-lined street connecting Placa de Catalunya that holds the Christopher Columbus Monument and a myriad of shops. That night they dined at the famous El Café De La Pedrera. Barcelona was magical. Jennifer was having the time of her life and Peter was enjoying every second of it as well. Just watching the looks on Jennifer's face was all he needed anyway. They rested a few days doing as little as possible. They just enjoyed each other's company. They cruised the countryside just to take in some of the ambiance of the country for a day and that evening packed for the next country.

The newlyweds were on to Italy. Their final stop would be Sorrento on the Amalfi Coast, but first Venice, the City of Canals and then Rome, the Eternal City.

The best word to describe their honeymoon, magnificent!

CONTI III
Change is Coming

Chapter 23

Ah, Venice, the city of canals. Jennifer and Peter coasted through them on the back of gondolas like they were a king and a queen and enjoyed it to the fullest. They truly weren't sure what they enjoyed the most on this exquisite trip but experiencing all of it together is what they got the most pleasure out of. The honeymoon was epic with more to come.

Rome was but a stepping-stone now before they wound up at their final destination, a magnificent villa on the Amalfi Coast.

Peter phoned ahead and had the villa prepared for occupancy. He was excited to go there for a number of reasons. He fell in love with the place the minute he saw it and now he was about to share this beautiful place with his new wife. He just hoped Jennifer would feel the same way. The fact that they would not be alone in a strange place was comforting to both. The Bansanos would see to that. Everything was going along absolutely flawlessly.

Peter had been in touch with his parents as they traveled. Theresa was enjoying the honeymoon almost as much as they were. When they were in Venice, Peter actually had a tentative schedule for the first time and informed his mom of it. He let her know they would be heading to Sorrento soon and he would phone her from there. She was anxious for details.

The happy couple arrived in Sorrento after a beautiful boat ride from Naples, their last stop after Rome. Jennifer's mouth dropped when she saw the villa. First and foremost, the view of the Mediterranean from the set of patios actually took her breath away. Magnificent does not cover it. The villa itself was not huge, but it definitely was not small either. It had four bedrooms and four baths and a kitchen to die for, with a balcony off of it. There was a patio deck holding a small pool outside the double glass doors leading out of the family room, both the balcony and the patio were perfectly placed looking over the sea. Magnificent.

Peter did not contact his new uncle immediately. The honeymoon wasn't over yet. They had a few places in the area they wanted to explore, and Peter didn't want the celebration of their marriage to end quite yet. He wanted Jenny all to himself for just a little while longer. They wanted to call and let them know they were there but decided to stay incognito for a number of days just enjoying the area and their new place. Peter wanted to be completely set up and buy a few things before he contacted his Uncle Gino, and, after that, it was just back to life. The first thing they bought was a car. So, they could move around freely. He was going to buy one for Jennifer as well, but she declined. One was enough for now was her reply. Next was a major purchase. Peter wanted a boat. Not a small boat and not too big of one. He ended up buying a 36-foot Sea Ray, the perfect size for entertaining, but still small enough to navigate without any problems. Their life in Sorrento was falling into place.

After they had accomplished what they wanted and were settled in, Peter called his Uncle Gino.

"Uncle Gino, we're here. We'll come by the restaurant tonight for dinner. Are you available to join us at say 7:00?"

"Yes, of course Peter, but Sofia and I would prefer you come to our home for dinner. I will prepare a feast to celebrate your marriage and your homecoming."

"Uncle Gino, there is no need for that."

"Sofia and I insist. We have been waiting for this call. You don't think we knew when you arrived? Of course, we did, we just thought you were on your honeymoon so we didn't want to bother you. We knew you would call when you were ready. In fact, we just missed by one day," he said laughing. Come early, the family is anxious to see you and my daughter Angelina is anxious to meet your Jennifer. Say 6:00.

"You know Uncle you always make me feel so welcome."

"That is because you are my nephew. See you tonight."

"Thank you. Can't wait to see you both. We have been looking forward to it."

"Us too. See you at 6:00."

Angelina was the first to greet them at the door. See couldn't wait to see her adopted cousin's new wife. She was not disappointed.

"Angelina, this is my wife Jennifer."

"Nice to meet you. My mother was right, you are a very beautiful woman," said Angelina in broken English.

"Funny, your mother said the same thing to me about you."

They both smiled and hugged. Sofia was right behind her daughter and hugged both Peter and Jennifer as soon as they were all the way in the house. Gino was next. Alberto, Angelina's boyfriend stood in the background but was hugged by Peter as well. Jennifer just shook his hand. They sat down, wine in hand and Jennifer was bubbling over explaining their trip. She left out very little and had all their attention the entire time. Even Peter was content as he listened. Just because he was so happy to hear what Jenny's opinion on the honeymoon was. To say she loved it would be one of the biggest understatements of all times.

The Bansanos asked about the new place and Peter invited them to come to breakfast the next morning to see their home away from home. The diner was great. Gino is a great cook, but Sofia is better. She outdid herself. Jennifer couldn't have been more comfortable around these people. They were just wonderful in every way. Sofia, as they ate, thanked Jennifer numerous times for the amazing way she was treated when visiting them for the wedding. It was one of if not the nicest time she had ever had. Gino said the same to Peter. He wanted to make sure he explained fully the bonding that took place between Peter's mom and dad and the Bansanos. He explained it best when he said, "They are part of our family now and we already miss them."

"I hope they will come to visit us here soon," answered Peter.

Sofia then said, "I hope a week from Saturday is not too soon for you, because they are coming then."

Peter just laughed when he heard that and said, "I could tell the last time we spoke Mom was anxious to come over. That is great news."

"I already told them at the restaurant that I would be gone for a while. I am looking forward to seeing your father again. I hope you will allow us to have time with them."

Peter laughed again and said, "I hope they will spend a little time with US."

They all laughed.

"Your brother Russell and his wife are also coming. Russell said to tell you, too bad."

Everyone laughed again.

"If you would like, your parents can stay here with us and your brother and his wife could stay with you at your home. But that is up to you. We are just offering," said Gino.

"No Uncle Gino. That will be whatever my father and mother say, but I'm sure they will probably split time at both our homes. How long did they say they were staying?"

"Thomas said ten days."

"Bene. Millie bene," said Peter. "All of this is good with you, isn't it sweetheart?"

"Perfect is the only word that comes to mind," she replied.

CONTI III
Change is Coming

Chapter 24

Peter, Jennifer, Gino, and Sofia waited patiently as the plane carrying the Contis arrived at the gate. Theresa was the first to come out of the tunnel door with Thomas and Russell following her, Colleen trailed the others but was closely behind. Theresa was smiling from ear to ear as she saw her son and his wife standing there. She smiled even bigger when she saw Sofia and said, "Oh my, this is unbelievable. I am so happy to see you all. Ciao, my family."

All four greeters stood waving as Peter yelled out, "Hi Mom."

Theresa hugged Jenny first, then Sofia. Peter was getting a hug from his father at the same time. Then Gino and Thomas hugged. It was a hug fest.

"Ciao mi familia, sono felice di essere qui, (hello family, I'm so happy to be here)," said a smiling Russell as he and Colleen joined in the hugging.

Jenny said to her new brother-in-law, "Wow, Russell, you surprised me with your Italian. Do you actually know what you were saying?"

Russell answered, "I think I said, hello family, I'm starving the food on the plane was terrible, but then again my Italian is not too good."

Everyone laughed.

Jenny then came back with, "No really, that was perfect Italian."

"Merci," said Russ.

"That's French," said a laughing Peter knowing his brother was kidding.

Everybody laughed again.

Gino then suggested, "I think maybe before we do anything we go to my restaurant, Buena Vista, for food. What you think Thomas? Theresa you hungry?"

"Great idea," said a smiling Russell.

And the laughing continued.

Sofia then pulled Theresa to the side and quietly asked, "Theresa we have much room at our house for you and Thomas if you want the young ones to stay together at Peter's. You are welcome if you like."

"Thank you, Sofia. Thomas and I have decided to stay the first half of our trip with our son, but we were hoping to stay the rest with you and Gino. If we are not imposing."

"You just made me and Gino happy. Mille grazzie."

"It is us that thank you. This is perfect," replied Theresa.

"After lunch at Uncle Gino's we can drop your stuff at the villa and then maybe a boat ride. The view from the water will take your breath away," said Peter.

"My brother. I'm already knocked out by what I've seen so far and that was from the plane. This place is magnificent."

"You haven't seen anything yet Russ. Family this place is paradise."

Thomas and Theresa hopped into Gino car and Russ and Colleen joined Peter and Jennifer in theirs. The trip of a lifetime for Peter's family was just getting started. Amalfi Coast here come the Contis.

When they walked into Gino's place, Theresa almost broke into tears. The restaurant, Buena Vista, meaning beautiful view, was situated on a point jutting out into the Mediterranean Sea and was the most beautiful spot Theresa had ever seen. All she could do was hug Sofia and say, "God has blessed you."

"Yes Theresa, he has. My friend from America has come to visit."

"You say the most wonderful thing. Thank you, thank you, Thank you."

"Enough talk. Let us all eat. The day is still young," said Gino. "I have already ordered for everyone. I'm sure you will like. Let's sit out on the balcony and enjoy the view."

Thomas patted Gino on the back and said, "Your place is magnificent my friend. Magnificent."

"Thank you, Thomas. My brother Vito certainly knew how to judge people. When he took Peter under his arm and, como se diche (how do you say), in his heart adopted him like a son, we were all enriched by it. Thomas, we are more than friends now, we are family.

Russell pulled Peter off to the side and just said, "Brother, I am so happy for you, I could cry."

"What's mine is your Russ. Always remember that."

"Thanks, but I'm already married to Colleen."

Peter through his arm around his brother's shoulders and just laughed.

Colleen stood at the side of the railing just gazing out over the Sea.

"It's beautiful isn't it?" Said Jenny.

"That just doesn't describe it. I'm awe struck. Thank you, Jenny, for inviting us."

"This isn't an invitation to visit. It's an open invitation to come whenever you want, if we're here or not. You're my sister now."

The two women hugged.

When they were through hugging Jenny turned to the family and said, "Wait until you see the villa."

Peter added, "It's nice guys."

After a wonderful lunch everyone, including the Bansanos headed over to Peter and Jenny's to drop off their luggage. The anxiety was killing them all.

They were not disappointed.

"Holy Shit," exclaimed Russell.

"Russell!" said Theresa loudly. "But Holy Cow."

"Wow son," added Thomas.

"Thanks Dad, the guest bedrooms are right there on that side of the great room. All the bedrooms have a view of the Sea. Pick one out and drop your stuff, you too Bro. Let's go to the boat. The view is pretty good here but the view from the water is, magnifico."

"Can't possibly be better, this view is the most beautiful I've ever seen," said Colleen.

"Well, Col, you haven't seen it from the Mediteranian." said Jenny with a smile.

They dropped their luggage like they were hot potatoes and before you knew it, they were loading onto Peter's new boat. Well actually it was a yacht, but not a big one. A boat becomes a yacht when the length reaches 32 feet. Peter's was 36 feet, the perfect size for 2 or 20.

Peter said to Gino as everyone climbed aboard, "Do you want to take the helm Uncle?"

"No, my nephew. You drive. I will point out things to your family. I am guide," he said with a smile.

The afternoon was perfect. The scenery was breath taking. Theresa said it was the best experience she ever had with her family and just wished that Marie could have been there. Peter, Jenny, Sofia, and Gino got every bit as much enjoyment just watching the looks on the faces of the Contis.

As they were docking Sofia said, "Please everyone if you are not too tired, I would love to have you come to our home for dinner."

"Sofia, we don't want to put you to any more trouble," answered Theresa.

"Having family to dinner is no trouble. It is my pleasure."

Gino injected, "Thomas, please come. We all have to eat."

"Dad, if you are too tired I understand, but Gino, Colleen and I happily accept your kind invitation."

"No one said we weren't going. Your mother and me can't wait to see Gino and Sofia's home. What time would you like us to be there Gino," asked Thomas.

"Whenever you are rested and ready. Anytime. We will drink wine and laugh when you get there."

Theresa turned to Sofia and asked, "What time Sofia, you are the one who is cooking?"

"Thank you, Theresa, Gino does not think food gets cold. Is 7:30 too early."

"Not at all. Do you want me to come early and help you cook?"

"Grazzi, no. Just come hungry," she answered with a smile.

      *   *   *

The entire trip was exactly like that and more for ten days. It was the best vacation of the entire family's lives.

There were hugs and tears at the airport when the Contis got ready to board the plane. It was the first but not the last time these people would be together in Italy, not by a long shot. The bonding was cemented. The Contis and the Bansanos were family, period. Three months ago, they didn't even know each other, now it was like they were family all their lives. Life was good for the Contis and for the Bansanos. Peter watched the emotional goodbye but felt happy. Happy that his Italian adventure, what with the Bansanos and buying a place there and all, worked out so great, but sad his family was leaving so soon. Jennifer watched too. She missed her new family already. As they disappeared into the doorway, Jennifer cried.

CONTI III
Change is Coming

Chapter 25

The next few months flew by. Everyday still felt like a honeymoon to the loving couple. But too much of a good thing can get a little old. Jennifer, whose days were filled with nothing but work for years was getting antsy.

"Peter, I'm loving every second of our life. This is not a complaint, but I need to do something besides just enjoying myself. Sorry, but it's true."

"What do you want to do? Our life is perfect."

"I know that, I was thinking about writing."

"Then write."

"Write what? Fiction, non-fiction, short stories, novels, I don't know."

"Sweetheart, whatever floats your boat."

"Peter, what kind of answer is that?"

"One that says you need to think about something like that before you jump in."

"Right. It's just a thought."

Peter responded with, "Jenny, I know exactly what you're saying though and I've given a little thought to it. I have actually thought about taking a long boat ride to the Puglia region."

"Where? And why?"

"I've been tossing around the idea of opening up a little business that you and I could get involved in. It would give us a reason to split our time up between the U.S. and Italy, and all in the name of business. You know we would be making business trips together to wherever. It's just a thought."

"Peter Conti, what have you done?"

"Jenny, did you know that more than one third of all olives are grown in Italy? There are more than 150 million olives trees growing in Italy today. Forty percent of the groves are in a region just east of here called the Puglia territory. Here's a little more about it. The territory of Puglia (pronounce apuglia in English) is on the easternmost coast and sits on a long narrow peninsula bordered by two seas, the Adriatic and the Lonion. It's fertile ground and ideal weather is perfect for growing olives and the groves are scattered throughout the region."

Jenny just smiled and said, "How long have you been doing research on this Mr. Encyclopedia Britannica?"

"Well. I guess we think alike. We need to do something besides," he just smiled and said, "naked time."

Jenny laughed out loud.

"What do you have in mind?"

"I was thinking of buying or buying into an olive grove and getting into the export business. Purglia is only about a three-hour drive from here. Together we could travel the world, sell olives and olive oil, use our creative minds, and make some money while we're doing it. What do you think?"

"You are something else Mr. Conti, really," she said smiling.

"Is that a yes?"

Jenny just kissed him as an answer.

"Then we can drive over there in our car, like I said it's only three hours, OR it's a two-day trip if we take a nice boat cruise. You decide."

"As long as the weather allows, let's take the boat."

"I love you Jennifer Conti."

"Diddo."

CONTI III
Change is Coming

Chapter 26

After a beautiful two-day cruise around the southwest point of Italy, the toe of the boot, which is the shape Italy is known for, the couple continued to the city that sits on the heel. Santa Maria di Leuca, Italy. Santa Maria is a beautiful city on the far south side of the Paglia region and is nestled right on the coast of the Adriatic Sea.

They docked the boat, rented a car, and started doing some due diligence on obtaining all or a portion of an olive farm. They were hoping to hook up with an operation that did more than just grow the olives. They needed one that besides growing them, sold the olives in bulk, packaged them, and processed them into refined products. It wouldn't be easy, and the better and bigger the business, the more it would cost.

Luck was on their side as they stumbled on an operation that was in need of working capital. The door was open. Not to buy it outright, because it wasn't for sale, but to invest and get equity. Peter worked a sweet deal and before you knew it. Peter and Jenny were part owners in a thriving olive oil operation. Perfect. The operation wouldn't change much, but there would be an addition attached. Santa Maria Olive Oil Company would add a new division, Santa Maria Exports.

It would take time, before the Contis would be able to put together an operation and a team to do most of the work, but they would oversee their end of the operation and make calls on the bigger players to build the personal relationships needed to make the endeavor a success. They both have the ware withal and the resumes to carry that out. That way they would have their fingers in the new operation but not full time. It was exactly what they both were looking for, interaction, prestige, and involvement, without major time consumption. After all, they weren't doing it for the money.

They drove the rental car back to their villa in Amalfi and made arrangements with Alberto, Angelina's fiancé, to drive the car back and skipper the boat home. It would be a nice little get away for his adopted cousin Angelina and her man, and as usual for Peter, win, win.

Everything was going along perfectly and then the phone rang.

"Orin. Man, it's nice to hear your voice. Please tell me you guys are coming to Italy for a visit."

"Peter, I wish that was the reason I'm calling. But my friend, it isn't."

"What happened?"

"It's bad Peter. It's Tully."

"Oh my God. Is he dead?"

"Not yet but according to all the Intel I've been able to gather. He's going to be."

"What are you talking about? What happened to him?"

"Tully has been captured by a terrorist group in Bakstana called The Azad. He's being held captive in a fortress outside of Beltran City. This Azad is a movement of religious and political fanatics that are in the mindst of taking over the government in Bakstana by the use of terrorism. A crazy man named Abu Musab Kalib is their leader. I've spoken to as many people as I can, all the way up the ladder, about getting him released, but it's the same mantra from everybody; we do not negotiate with terrorist. Peter, Tell's as good as dead."

"Holy shit Orin, what are you planning on doing about it? I know you."

"Peter, I already contacted Nitro and Lavaca. We're going to get him out. That's why I'm calling. Buddy, I know you just got married but John Tully is going to die if we don't do something. I don't exactly know how we're going to get him out of there, but I'm putting the team back together. Are you in or out?"

"Jesus Christ Orin. I owe the guy many times over, you know that; he saved my ass and I mean plenty of times. I can't let him die without trying. This is going to be hard for Jennifer to swallow, but I'm in."

"I have a call in for the Secretary of State Thomas Pearl. I don't know what he can do for us. I'm pretty sure I'll have to get you and LaVaca reinstated. Everything is up in the air, but time is of the essence. I need you back home buddy, and pronto."

"Where do you need me and when?"

"I'll call you back as soon as I hear from The Secretary, but I'm thinking Washington, D.C. in less than a week. Can you make it?"

"I'll be there when you need me. Jesus Christ Orin. Jesus Christ."

"I hope he comes with you buddy, we're gonna need him."

Jenny walked into the room just as Peter hung up the phone. The look on his face must have said it all.

"What happened?" She asked almost frantically.

"Jennifer, I need to go back to the states. You can stay here if you like, but I need to get back."

"Peter, what are you talking about? Did someone die?"

"Not yet, it's John Tully, one of our team. He's been imprisoned somewhere in the Middle East and he's about to. That was Orin, he wants to break him out."

"Break him out of prison. The Middle East. One of your Green Beret team. Sweetheart, that was years ago. Break him out of prison. What prison? When? How?"

"Jenny, this is not up for discussion."

"Not up for discussion. Are you kidding me Peter? This is our life you're talking about."

"I KNOW! Do you think I wanted this to happen? I love you Jenny more than you could ever imagine, but I owe this man my life. Orin, Nitro, and LaVaca are going to do this and I will not let them do it alone. I can't. I couldn't live with myself if anything were to happen to those guys and I wasn't there to help or maybe even stop it."

Jenny started to cry. She stopped herself, pulled herself together, took a deep breath, and said, "I understand. I'll start to pack."

She walked out of the room looking like she just lost her best friend. Her fear was that maybe she was going to.

CONTI III
Change is Coming

Chapter 27

Seventy-two hours later, Orin, Betty, Nitro, Sally, and the unmarried Joe LaVaca sat in the lobby of the D.C. Hilton awaiting the arrival of Peter and Jenny. As soon as they entered Joe got up and hugged Peter.

"Long time no see my friend," said LaVaca.

"I'm sorry it's under these circumstances buddy," answered Peter.

"No kidding."

"Joe, this is my wife Jennifer, Jenny."

"Pleasure to meet you Jenny. So sorry I missed your wedding. I was out of the country and wasn't able to attend. Our friends have told me what a wonderful woman you are. They also mentioned you were pretty. They were wrong. Beautiful would be much closer to the truth."

"Thank you, Mr. LaVaca. What a wonderful thing to say and a perfect way to meet someone who is so important to my husband."

Joe turned around looking and then turned back and said, "Is my father here? My father's name is Mr. LaVaca. My name is Joe, Jenny."

Everyone was laughing at the exchanged while they waited their turn to hug the new arrivals.

The conversation that was about to happen was going to be a very serious discussion that the men really didn't want the women to be privy too. Not that it was a secret; the men just didn't want them to worry any more than they already were. Betty suggested that the three ladies stroll over to the bar for a before dinner drink or two. The men sat and talked.

"Now that we're all here, this is what we're facing. A group of militant gorilla fighting terrorist, led by Abu Musab Kalib, invaded the Bakstana Government Office in an attempt to take over the government. They already occupied a major section of Beltran City, the Capitol. Tully, and a small force he commanded, were able to get the Prime Minister, Ahmad Farouk, to safety, but while doing so he and a few of his men were captured. Kalib is now demanding all American troops out of Bakstana and he wants Ahmad Farouk to relinquish control of the country to the government of the Azad, or else the Americans are dead. We are meeting with Sec. State Thomas Pearl at 0900 hours tomorrow morning to discuss what can be done. We've had a few conversations and in every one of them he mentioned whatever is done will not be sanctioned by our government and we're going to be disavowed of any connection with the U.S.A. Basically we'll be on our own as far as they are claiming BUT make no mistake this is a military action."

Peter injected, "How can that be with me and Joe already discharged?"

"Reinstatement."

"How?" asked Joe.

"We'll work that out tomorrow, but I already informed Sec. State Pearl that the reinstatement will be at the same rank as Nitro and Tully, maybe even me. I'm willing to take the demotion so we don't have a ranking officer on the mission."

"Majors?" asked a surprised ex-Captain Joe LaVaca. "Nice."

"Does it matter?" replied Orin.

"Not really," answered Joe.

"Guys, I hope I didn't open my mouth and stick my foot in it because the stakes are our lives," said Orin.

"If you didn't Orin, Tell and his men are goners," injected Peter.

Nitro then asked Orin, "Do you have a plan?"

"I've put some thought to it, but not really guys. Not until we see how much support we're getting from Uncle Sam."

"Then we'll find out in the morning won't we," replied Nitro.

"Right," said Peter. Then Peter turned to Joe and said, "By the way, where the fuck have you been for Christ sakes?"

"Industrial information gatherer."

All three guys laughed, and Orin blurted out, "You're a fucking INDUSTRIAL SPY?"

"Well, some people may call it that, but I prefer to call it an information gatherer."

The guys laughed again.

Joe came back with, "But, what I'm about to say is very important for our cause. It surely will come in handy. I've been working the Middle East on and off for 4 years. Guys, I speak Farsi."

"No shit. Joe, that's big," said Peter.

LaVaca just smiled and said, "I know."

Nitro suggested that they were away from the women long enough and that they should join them in the bar. They got up to leave. Joe grabbed Peter by the arm as they were walking out and pulled him aside. "Pete, first I didn't hear about Jackie for months after the tragedy. I was sick for you my brother. I would have been there if I was in the country. You know that, right?"

"Of course, Joe. Thanks though, it was a tough time in my life."

"I'm happy for you now, Pete. Congratulations."

"Thanks pal, never thought lightning could strike twice in one man's life but God works in mysterious ways."

"Let's get Tell and his men home, and you back to your bride. Then we'll party until the cows come home."

The two men hugged and went into the lounge for a drink with the rest of their party.

They were all smiles as the reunion went on, but it was definitely different. The difference was every one of them knew why they were there. Danger was not a big enough word to cover the situation. These men were putting their lives on the line, for their comrade at arms. The women were scared to death. The men knew it was something they had to do. John T. Tully needed them, and they were not going to let him down. Not without a hell of a fight. All four men knew the man they called Tell, would do the same for them.

Tomorrow was going to be a very important day.

CONTI III
Change is Coming

Chapter 28

The next morning Peter and his Green Beret team sat in a conference room at the White House waiting for Thomas Pearl, the Secretary of State to arrive. Five minutes later, he, along with the Secretary of Defense, General Curt Grothmann, entered the palatial room.

"Good morning soldiers," was the first word out of the distinguished man's mouth. "I'd like to introduce myself. I am sure you are aware I am Secretary of State, Thomas Pearl and this is General Curtis Grothmann, our Secretary of Defense."

Orin spook for the group, "Of course we know and we're sorry we are meeting under these trying circumstances, otherwise it would be a pleasure. I'm also aware that you gentlemen know who we all are by name but still let me introduce you to each man on our team. As you are well aware, or we wouldn't be here each of us have a specific skill set. Before I start the introductions though, I would like to ask if the reinstatement and promotion paperwork for Peter Conti and Joseph LaVaca has been okayed?"

"Yes Colonel, everything you asked for in those regards has been approved," answered General Grothmann.

"Good. And have I been demoted to major?"

"Temporarily Sir," responded the General, with a smile. "Unusual request Colonel."

"Not really. This is a team of equals and no one is in command. We will be running this OP from the seat of our pants. Formality has no place in it."

"Alright, MAJOR, we understand," added Pearl.

"Okay then, on my right is Major Nigel (Nitro) Burke, best explosive man in the man's army. Next to him sits Major Peter Conti, he could shoot the eye out of a snake from a thousand yards, guaranteed. This is Major Joseph LaVaca, the ghost. I think that explains his skill. He also is fluent in Farsi. You know who I am. My job is to coordinate these experts into the well-oiled machine they are. Sirs, these men are the best of the best. If we didn't think we could accomplish this mission, we wouldn't be here. We are willing to risks life and limb to bring Major Tully and his men home. Our question to you is. What will you do to help us accomplish that mission?"

"Gentleman, all military equipment and staff are at your disposal, you are Priority One. From here on out you will go by the handle of GB Team Alpha and have the full cooperation from all military bases, until you enter Bakstana that is. From there you're on your own. We can't risk an all-out war in the region if we get involved militarily. That's why we have to disavow any actions you men will take. We stand behind you all the way in our hearts but legally and politically, we just can't."

"Understand Sir," answered Orin. "As I said we will be flying by the seat of our pants, but our objective is clear. From the Intel we have, our men are being held in a complex on the outskirts of Beltran City. We know they house soldiers and train men at the facility as well and we know that often times Abu Musab Kalib is present there. Our plan is to get our men out and blow the entire complex to smithereens, hopefully killing the head of the snake when we do. We'll need access of course but we'll have to work that out on the fly. We can fly into our base in Saudi Arabia, supply ourselves there with all the necessary equipment we'll need and try like hell to get in to Bakstana without being seen, blow up the complex, and get out with our men. That's all we have for a plan until we see the terrene and the battle forces we'll be facing.

"Colonel, I mean Major. I must say Orin I'm not crazy about the demotion decision, but it's yours to make, we know what we're asking you men to do. Don't think for a moment we're throwing you to the wolves. We here know your background and your accomplishments. If we didn't think it was possible, we wouldn't have gone along with this, but what this team and what you men were able to achieve in Vietnam, you has the respect of every one of us in Washington. If it can be done, we think you men are the men to do it," said a confident Secretary of Defense.

"Thank you General," answered Orin. "We know time is of the essence and we'd like to get started as soon as possible."

With that said, the door to the conference room opened and in stepped George Fowler, the President of the United States. All the men in the room stood. Orin and team along with the General, saluted.

"At ease men. I just wanted to meet these brave men and thank them in person for the challenge they're about to undertake."

He shook each of their hands and when he came to Peter he stopped and said, " Peter, I knew when I met you, you were some kind of soldier, never thought I'd be witnessing it myself. Thank you, sir, for coming when your country needs you." He finished shaking hands and was departing. As he left, he said, "I'd stay but honestly I don't want to hear any of this. Politics you know. It makes it hard to do your job. One more thing, Peter say hello to Jennifer for me. If she's still talking to me after this." With that he was gone.

The men finished acquiring the contact list they needed in Saudi Arabia, along with contacts in the Bakstana underground that have agreed to help them maneuver in their country. They all shook hands and the Secretaries wished them good luck. They were scheduled to be on a flight to Saudi Arabia the next night. **It just got real.**

CONTI III
Change is Coming

Chapter 29

GB Team Alpha stayed in the conference room to talk over what had just transpired. Before anyone said a thing, Joe spoke up, "Jesus Christ Peter. You know the President?"

"Not me. My wife. I guess you didn't know but Jenny was a Congress Women and she was also the Ambassador to the Soviet Union before we got married."

"What. I thought she was Miss America," he said jokingly.

"I told you Joe. I hit the lottery with Jenny."

"No kidding!"

Orin interrupted, "She's very nice. Now back to business. Let's hear your thoughts of what we were just told. What did you like about what was said and what didn't you like?"

Joe immediately said, "I love the part about being promoted to Major. Thanks Orin."

"That was a nice, thanks buddy, but why and how did you pull that off?" added Peter.

"You heard what I said about no bosses. We need to improvise as we go. Not follow orders that might not fit the situation. I know we could have just ignored ranks but what the hell. You guys are Majors. It can't hurt."

"I didn't get shit out of it. I'm already a Major."

"And a damn good one Nitro," answered Orin. "There you go, you just got a compliment."

All four guys laughed.

Then the serious questions started to flow. Starting with Peter. "What kind of recon do we have on the area?"

"Satellite shots of where the insurgent bases are and plenty of photos of the terrain shots and the City of Beltran. Good ones. What I see is a few ways we can bypass the fighters and navigate through the jungle to get to the river. The Huzah River will be how we get in and out. How we do that, I don't know yet, but I'm all ears if any of you have any idea," answered Orin.

Joe injected, "They said we have connections with the Bakstana underground, right. I'm thinking they would have to have some kind of boat or whatever, but some way to travel the river."

"I'm sure that can be worked out," answered Orin.

"Look we have all day tomorrow before we take off and plenty of time in the air to scrutinize the satellite shots, study the Saudi Arabia base info, and put together what equipment we think we're going to need. After throwing ideas at each other we will come up with something, at least a starting point," said Peter. "I suggest we spend time with the women tonight. I don't know about Sally and Betty, but Jenny is scared to death. We need to make this sound like it's a walk in the park. They're going to worry enough. Let's not talk about it at all."

"Good thinking Peter," said Orin. "I've got a few ideas already, but four heads are better than one. And you're right Betty is petrified and usually she's as cool as a cucumber about my military work."

"Sally too. Let's just have a nice dinner together and hit the rack early. I doubt if we'll get much rest over there," added Nitro.

The four were in agreement and they left to go back to the hotel. It was just before noon when they walked into the lobby and found the three women talking in the sitting area of the lobby.

"Hi Betty, Sal, Jenny," said Orin. Peter and Nitro simultaneously followed by an additional, "hi honey," from Peter.

The women were not smiling. In fact, with a serious look on her face Betty, obviously their spokesperson blurted out, "We want to know exactly what's going on. You constantly keep us in the dark. Normally that's not a problem, but this is different. We think we have a right to know what the hell is going on here."

Peter turned to his cohorts and said, "Guys, they're right. If you don't mind, I'll tell them without breaking any confidentiality of today's meeting."

"All yours my friend," said Orin.

"Here it is in a nutshell. Tully and three of his men are in prison and we're going to get them out. There now you know."

"We already knew that Peter," said a stern looking Jenny.

"Wait, let me finish," continued Peter with both hands held up like someone was holding a gun on him. "The four of us have faced ten times more danger than something like this. We're not even going to have to go inside the place. We've got Nitro Burke. We blow out the wall, grab the men, and were gone. It's a piece of cake."

"Why you men then Orin," said Betty.

"Honey, you know we don't talk about this stuff, but there's two main reasons. One, because this is a job for a small stealth group, that's what we are, and we're the best, that's not bragging, that's fact. Two, its Tully we're talking about here. John Tully saved all of our lives

185

numerous times. We are not about to let him rot in some prison for simply doing his duty. We know it's a little dangerous. We're sorry to put you women through this, but it has to be done and we're going to do it. You knew who you married. Let us be that person. We never talk about it, but you have no idea what kind of heroes these three guys standing next to me are. Trust me they know what they're doing."

Nitro added, "Four."

"Sorry ladies. There is no other option. The hardest part is getting there. The rest we've done dozens of times. I'd say don't worry, but we all know you will. Betty, Sally, I promise Joe and I will protect these old men," said Peter.

"Old men. Why don't you say that to my face," said Orin knowing Peter was trying to change the mood.

"Just in case you get lucky and land a punch to this almost perfect face of mine."

Orin responded with, "Obviously, you don't own a mirror."

The four men laughed a hearty laugh. Even the women smiled. The talk was over. It didn't stop the women from worrying, but it helped a little.

"Let's all go have lunch. I'm buying," said LaVaca.

"What? You're buying? This has got to be a first. There has to be a reason behind this," said Nitro.

"Well, I'm pretty smart so I figure, lunch will be a lot less than the dinner bill. I'll be out of that argument."

"What if we don't have dinner together tonight? Did you even think of that?" asked Orin.

"SON OF A BITCH!" responded Joe.

Everyone just laughed.

Mission accomplished thought Joe.
The afternoon and evening was pleasant for all. They had a wonderful time sightseeing that afternoon. Jenny was the guide, after all she knew the town like the back of her hand. They went places you have to be somebody to go to. The group was impressed.

After dinner they all went back to their rooms. It was time to be alone. The woman prayed that this wouldn't be the last time.

CONTI III
Change is Coming

Chapter 30

The next morning flew by. The three wives had discussed staying together until their husbands returned but decided that going back to their normal life would help keep their minds off of what their husbands were doing. They would still be worried, but not 24/7 like they would be if they were together and constantly talking about it.

The couples individually went to the airport. This needed to be a private goodbye for each of them. Just in case.

Jenny stood face to face with Peter just before she boarded. She didn't cry. She knew she needed to be brave and not make this parting something too sad. They were hugging and as much as she tried not to, tears welled up in her eyes. They kissed and as their lips parted, she said, "Please come back to me."

"Jenny, I never make promises that I can't keep so listen closely. I promise, I will come home to you. God wouldn't have put us together if he didn't want us to be together. I love you Jennifer Taylor Greer Conti, with all my heart."

"I love you more," she replied.

With a giant smile on his face he said, "You can't. That would be impossible."

They kissed again and she was gone.

Two hours later GB Team Alpha was sitting in the situation room at the Pentagon going over the Intelligence they were given on Abu Musab Kalib. They were told that he was at the prison complex as they spoke, but no one knew for exactly how long.

They all scrutinized the satellite photos to get an overview of what faced them. What they saw was that Beltran City sat on a giant oasis in the middle of nowhere. The city existed solely because of the supply of water flowing from the Huzah River. There were hills surrounding the city due to the unusual terrain formed by the river.

Peter said as he regurgitated the information, "These hills surrounding the city will definitely aid our cause. They should provide plenty of cover for us to get to the outskirts of the city. But, getting in position to attack the complex is another story."

"No one said this was going to be easy," said Orin. "Let's talk about what we're going to do as soon as we hit the ground. Here's my thoughts, we take two assault vehicles both with 50 caliber machine guns mounted on them from the Riyadh Air Base* in Saudi Arabia, to the boarder of Bakstana. From there, with the help of the Bakstana underground, we travel the 80 miles to the river, hoping to avoid any meetings with Azad gorilla fighters of course. If we do, we'll have to deal with it, thus the 50 cals. From there we hit the river. Again, we'll need the underground connections for help and support there. They must have people who run that river. Until we get there, we won't know exactly what we're dealing with."

"Give us the what ifs Orin or at least what you think we will be facing," asked Peter.

"Guys, we'll be in danger from the moment we hit Bakstana soil. I don't need to tell you that. If we get to the river, we'll be facing another unknown. The river is canvassed by numerous Azad water patrols. They took over the river waterway when they invaded the Capital and ousted Ahmad Farouk, the Prime Minister."

Nitro spoke up, "So far you're making this sound like it's doable until you got to the river part. We're going to be sitting ducks."

"That we have to play by ear. We'll have to be in disguise of course. If we're boarded it's kill or be killed. The river travel will be something we have to chance. It could cause us great grief, more than great grief guys, maybe our lives."

Joe then said, "You're not making this sound too safe, buddy."

"That ain't the half of it. If we live through the river portion, we have to navigate our way through the city, with all our equipment, set up, break out our men from a heavily guarded prison complex, and escape the same way we came in."

"Oh, I thought this was going to be difficult," joked Peter.

Orin continued, "I've seen what you men can do. We can do this. It will take a ton of cooperation from the Bakstana underground, but if they want to get their country back, they'll surely do all they can. Nitro and his toys will help them with their cause."

"I'll tell you this," answered Nitro. "That complex will not be the same after we're out of there. I just hope Kalib and a bunch of the uppity ups of the Azad are there when we get there because if they are, they won't be breathing when we leave."

* Riyadh Air Base is one of the most important Air Bases in the American repertoire because it's strategically located smack dab in the middle of the Middle East, giving the American troops the chance to easily support any potential invasion in the area.

Orin spoke again "I'd love to blow that son of a bitch Kalib to hell, but that's not our main objective. Getting our men home is. Remember that!"

"Understood Orin," said Peter. "But if I get eyes on that bastard, I'll put a round between his eyes. Count on that. Just for Tully and the Bakstana people."

"Sounds good but try not to jeopardize the operation Peter. We all want that piece of shit dead, but our men come first."

"Got it," answered Peter. "Okay, do you have any kind of plan to work our way through the city, if we do get that far, that is?"

Orin answered, "I thought we were all going to contribute to this plan?"

"Orin, we will improvise on the spot, but this is your bailiwick. Just keep going," said Peter.

Orin continued with, "All depends on what kind of help we'll get from the underground. We'll definitely need their help getting us into position. We just have to stay close to these guys, without them we'll stick out like a sore thumb. It shouldn't be that difficult. That's not the problem I foresee, the big problem is transporting the weapons and our equipment. That's what I'm worried about. We're going to need the undergrounds help with that too, for sure."

Joe then said, "And you said the river was going to be dangerous. Are you saying all we'll have for weapons when we're moving through the city are our side arms?"

Orin answered, "If we run into trouble they'll have to do. We'll just have to fight our way out and abandon the mission. If we get split up, we'll meet at the rendezvous spot at the awaiting escape boat. It should be in the same place that dropped us off."

Nitro says, "What about Tully?"

"Nigel, we're only four guys without weapons, other than a couple of 45's apiece. We won't have a choice," answered Orin.

"God Damn," said Nitro shaking his head.

"We'll make it to the complex. There's no reason for us to be stopped. Let's think positive and go from there," said an optimistic Orin. "When we get to the complex, that's when we'll have to improvise."

Peter nodded his head in agreement and said, "We'll have to cross that bridge when we come to it."

That was that. It was the semblance of a plan. Too many variables to contend with so what they temporarily had was going to have to do.

There were other people in the room while the team discussed their plan who were basically just observing, so they would have some idea what these guys were attempting to do. Not just anybody. General Grothmann and Thomas Pearl were two of the observers. They were totally impressed to say the least. To say the most, they both started believing that these four extraordinary men could pull this thing off. They originally had their doubts because of the enormous undertaking they were asking these men to do, but everything they heard seemed plausible. Make no mistake, they both realized that things could go wrong all along the line, but they had confidence in these men. They knew what they were able to accomplish numerous times in Viet Nam and many of the missions were near impossible. These were not just average solders. They were special and these two men knew it. As the meeting broke up and GB Team Alpha was preparing to leave for their flight, General Grothmann and Thomas Pearl shook their hands and wished them luck.

There was but one thought running through both of these distinguished gentlemen's heads about these men. It wasn't really a thought it was a word, and the word was RESPECT.

CONTI III
Change is Coming

Chapter 31

GB Team Alpha's transport landed at Riyadh Miltary Base at 0400 hours. They slept a little on the flight, but mostly just kept going over possible angles to extract Tully and his men while doing major damage to the Azad. If at all possible, end the rein of Kalib before it really starts. Once on the ground they reported to Colonel Ronna Ashan, a West Point graduate and fellow Viet Nam veteran who is now the base commander at Riyadh.

"GB Team Alpha reporting for duty Colonel," said now Major Olsen.

"Welcome Majors. I've been kept abreast of your mission and have been told to assist you in every way I can. I'm truly happy to oblige. I'm not really sure I feel comfortable letting you go into Bakstana alone though. We have a full complement of American soldiers here, but as I've been told this is a non- sanctioned mission. It's not my call. Politics are crazy in the Middle East is all I can say. What do you need from me?"

Orin gave him a list of equipment they put together on the flight which included, two hand held missile launchers, two jeeps mounted with 50 caliber machine guns, two hand held 50 caliber rifles, two long rang assault sniper rifles, two hand held machine guns, eight 45 caliber hand guns with shoulder holsters, a dozen hand grenades, and a dozen M-14 riffles. The M-14's were for the team, any members of the underground who were assisiting, and for the escapees.

"Are you expecting trouble Major," joked the Colonel.

"It's possible Colonel," answered Orin.

"No problem men. I'll put this together immediately. Anything else?"

"We'll need Arab clothing as well. If we're going to be disavowed, we might as well be labeled spies."

"As I mentioned, I'm not too happy how this is being handled, but I've been told your team is ready willing and able to carry out this mission."

"Yes Sir. We'll get it done. One thing more Colonel," said Orin as he turned to Nitro, "Nitro give the Colonel your list of the explosives and equipment you need."

"Here you go Colonel. I think we can do some damage to the Azad with this stuff."

"You are some scary men Majors is all I can say."

"Thank you, Sir," was Orin's response with a smile.

"Good Luck men. Bring our soldiers home."

"Yes Sir," was the simultaneous response from GB Team Alpha.

"Before you leave there is someone you need to be introduce to."

With that said a virile looking Arab man entered the Colonel's office.

Colonel Ashan then said, "Gentlemen this is Jamaal Geshal, the leader of the Bakstana underground. He has agreed to help you in any way he can."

"As-salaam alaykum (peace be upon you)," said Jamaal.

LaVaca answered for the group, "Wa-alaykum as-salaam (peace be upon you, too.)

Jamaal continued with, "I speak English. I went to College in the United States. I am Jamaal Geshal and I am at your service Majors. My countrymen and I thank you for your help. Anything that hurts the Azad helps our cause."

"Jamaal Geshal, I am Orin Olsen, this is Peter Conti, Joe LaVaca here is our man who speaks Farsi, and this man is Nitro Burke, explosives expert. Believe me the pleasure is ours. We are in desperate need of you and your organizations help. Have you been briefed on the mission?"

"Yes, Major Olsen."

"From this moment on it will be first names, I'm Orin. There is no formality here."

"Good Orin, we will be fighting next to each other very soon. Formality does not fit."

"Agreed, Jamaal, I'm Peter."

"Joe."

"Nitro."

"Now that that's out of the way. We need to talk. We have a semi-plan we think can work, but not without your assistance. Colonel if you can direct us to a conference room, we can go over it. Any ideas you may have just blurt them out. Nothing is cut in stone," said Orin to Jamaal and Colonel Ashan.

The Colonel led them to a nice conference room but not before he gave the list of everything GB Team Alpha needed equipment wise, to his orderly and said he needed everything on that list pronto. The six men sat and looked at the satellite photos and Orin went through the plan he and the other members of the team came up with. Jamaal listened intently before he spoke,

"It is the distance we must travel from the Saudi/Bakstana boarder to Telerude, the city where we will be entering the river, that we have to worry about. The Azad have many camps sprinkled throughout and we could run into them at any time. This is a problem. The river trip could be less of a problem because we have good loyal people located along the way. They have fishing boats and travel and fish all along the river from Telerude to Beltran City. Even though the Azad have patrol boats that cruise the river, they are used to seeing the fishing boats of our friends. I say that it could be less dangerous, but you never know.

"Will you be traveling with us?"

"Of course."

"How many men will you bring with you?"

"I have a partner and trusted friend who is coming and two more will meet us when we get to Telerude."

Orin continued with, "Once we get off the boat, we need to traverse the city to get to the Azad complex. We need our equipment there as well. How do you suggest we get that accomplished?"

Jamaal answered, "We have many insurgents that follow our cause, I can arrange for the equipment to be where you want. We should be able to make our way thru the city streets if you are dressed for it. Just stay close to us. We will be pushing empty food carts looking like we have already sold our goods and are heading back to replenish our supply. Just keep your heads down and do not talk to one another. We have many people loyal to our government, but too many who side with the Azad. Do not take the chance that one of them will hear you speak English."

"Understood," replied Orin. "Do you need supplies, weapons or anything else?"

"We have limited weapons, but we have some."

"Not any more Jamaal. Colonel, we'll need to beef up our equipment list and also we need another jeep with a 50 cal loaded on top for Jamaal and his men."

"What ever you need. Just write it down and I'll add it to the list."

"Thank you Colonel," said Orin.

"No, thank you, all of you. If you're successful you can put an end to a war that hasn't even started."

"How soon will it take to fill that list?" asked Peter.

"We'll have it ready later today," answered the Colonel.

Orin turned to Jamaal and asked, "Can you and your man be ready in the morning? Our Intel tells us Kalib is at the complex, but we don't know for how long."

"Yes. No problem."

"Will you be able to put things in order with your people on the river and in Beltran City that fast?" asked Orin.

"Everything will be in place. We just need the Azad to cooperate," Jamaal said with a smile.

Peter, Nitro, and Joe listened intently to everything being said and had nothing more to add that Orin didn't cover. They were ready.

Abu Musab Kalib, GB Team Alpha is coming and they're bringing hell fire with them.

CONTI III
Change is Coming

Chapter 32

Bright and early the next morning everything was set for the assault. Jamaal and his trusted friend and underground partner Kareem Abdul Fasad were sitting in one of the combat jeeps and were ready to go. Jamaal would man the gun if and when trouble was to occur. Peter and Orin were in the lead vehicle; Peter would grab the turret on that one, and defending the rear, was the combat jeep driven by Nitro, shooting was Joe's duty. It was two hours to the boarder. That was just an almost leisurely drive through the country of Saudi Arabia compared to what was possible when they crossed into Bakstana. All eyes would be on the lookout for Azad militia the second they enter Bakstana they could be anywhere.

Peter was studying the satellite map photos as they drove. They showed areas that could be crawling with the enemy. Peter asked Orin to take a look. The three machines stopped together to servile the areas once again. Jamaal suggested a slight turn to the north to bypass one such area. They could travel north just a short way and then back south again to meet up with their original route. It seemed to have worked out, but ten miles past where they turned back they just about ran smack dab into another patrol, but were lucky enough to spot them before they were spotted themselves. Orin stop the small caravan and the men exited the vehicles.

Joe said, "Before we do anything, let me sneak up over that dune and do some recon."

Orin responded with, "Take Peter with you and take a couple of sniper rifles. If there are only a few of them, take them out."

"Roger that," answered both men.

They were gone and back in half an hour.

"Well," said Nitro before Orin got a chance to ask.

Peter answered, "Too many for the two of us. One or two of them could get away and warn the others. We need to surround them and take them out like we did on the Fong Lo Peak mission. It looks like their cooking and getting ready for a meal. I think all of them are together. We didn't see any guards."

"Is there enough cover to do that?" asked Orin.

"Yes and no," answered Joe. "We'll have to low crawl a bit."

"Let's go before while they're still all together," injected Nitro.

Jamaal asked, "What do you want us to do?"

Orin answered, "If any one of them are able to escape it's pretty certain they will head towards the camp we skirted. Cut them off and take them out. We can't afford to lose our element of surprise. If they warn Kalib, he'll be gone."

"Understand," said Jamaal.

Within minutes the four Americans were on the move. They split up and moved to encircle the band of Azad soldiers. Peter was in the lead because the area he was moving to had the best angle of attack. They all can shoot, but not like Peter. When Peter was in position he would signal with the use of a mirror flashing in the sun. The other three were to get ready and would fire as soon as they heard Peter take his first shot.

Boom, the first Azad soldier went down. Then all hell broke lose. When the smoke cleared the enemy lay dead. War is hell.

The team regrouped and as they did they heard two shots. Obviously one of the Azad men was able to escape the ambush, but not for long. Jamaal saw to that.

They were aboard their jeeps again and heading towards Telerude. It was clear sailing until they were about ten miles from the river. The team ran into two members of the Jamaal's underground who had scouted the route they knew Jamaal and the Americans would have to take to get to Telerude. They were waiting for them. These men were also part of the crew of the fishing boat that would take them on the Huzah Riverto to Beltran City.

"Jamaal," shouted one of them as he flagged down the small caravan. "There is a guard outpost manned by three members of the Azad two miles ahead, located in a pass that guards the entrance to Telerude. We didn't know what to do. We were afraid to kill them thinking that would give away our intensions. What do you want us to do?" Asked one of the brave members of the Bakstana underground.

Jamaal turned to the Americans and asked, "Gentlemen, how do you want to handle this?"

"I assume the underground and the Azad have been in many skirmishes, said Orin. "Is there a way we can take out the guards and blame it on your people? Do your people leave some kind of symbolic calling card when they secretly attack? You are in the midst of an internal war I'm sure you've had your share of battles. I'm not trying to push it off on your people but we need to get to Beltran City without anyone knowing we're coming. The element of surprise is our best weapon."

"Yes, we throw pig's blood on the Azad dead. That way they can not get to the promised land and get their 40 virgins. They know it is the underground that does this."

"Where are we going to get pig's blood?" asked Peter.

"Any blood will do, they do not know the difference," answered Jamal.

"That will work," said Joe. "Let me and Peter take care of this."

"Get it done," said Orin.

"Understood," replied Peter.

They drove to within a mile of the small out post. Peter and Joe took off. An hour later they were back.

"It's done," said Peter.

"Ishmal, the underground member who gave the warning said, "We have boats just outside of the city waiting for orders Jamaal. We are ready."

"Take us there Ishmal and good work. Thank you my friend."

Three hours later the Bakstana team and GB Team Alpha were loading and stowing their equipment on the larger of the fishing boats.

"So far so good," said Nitro. "But what about the Azad patrols canvassing the river. What's the plan if we are stopped?"

"There's the problem. "What did I say about nobody saying this was going to be easy. If we get in a battle on the water, we're just going to have to act fast and furious."

GB Team Alpha was almost half way to their goal. If they can travel the river without being detected the objective becomes that much more doable. Time will tell.

Not long into the journey, an Azad patrol boat slid dangerously close to their fishing boat. Ishmal waved a friendly hello. Obviously one of the Azad soldiers recognized Ishmal and waved a hello back, so far so good. Ten miles up the river they weren't so lucky.

Another patrol boat came by, this time one of the soldiers yelled for Ishmal to pull the boat over. They were about to be boarded.

There were six armed men standing on the front of the patrol boat getting ready to board when Peter jumped out from behind the doorway leading down to the cargo hold. He was holding an automatic machine gun. Joe was right behind him holding the same. The Americans let loose and sprayed the bow of the patrol boat with led. All six Azad fell dead. The driver of the boat immediately took off to try and escape. Peter jumped from the fishing boat onto the patrol boat before it got clear. The driver took two shots from his pistol at Peter before Peter was able to put a round into the man's face. The boat was then running out of control, but Peter was able to grab the wheel and shut it down before it crashed into the shoreline.

Ishmal guided the fishing boat over to Peter and Peter yelled out, "I'll pull this boat into the small cove right there. We can cover it and get it hid, but let's do it fast and get out of here."

They did exactly that, leaving the bodies piled up in the hold of the patrol boat. They were on there way again in minutes.

"That was close," said Jamaal.

"Peter and Joe are bad to the bone," replied Orin.

Jamaal came back with, "You can say that again."

That was the only encounter that they had on the entry run, but getting there was the easy part. Getting back would be a whole lot different. The Azad will be looking for them on the way back if they succeed in their mission.

They landed and hid the boat near the city's edge. There was about a half a mile or so to go before they were actually in the city itself. Ishmal had a number of food carts sitting and waiting at the landing site that had false bottoms in them, a perfect way to transport the equipment. Orin, Peter, Nitro, Joe, Jamaal, and Kareem would travel in groups of three pushing the carts so they wouldn't be that noticeable. Orin, Peter, and Kareem were in one group and Jamaal led the others.

With a little luck, their goal was in reach.

Conti III
Change is Coming

Chapter 33

They moved through the city without being noticed and stopped at the spot on the satellite map that they designated for their starting point. It was well hidden from view of the complex and out of the main thoroughfare. Two of the crew of the fishing boat Habib and Mohamad, left the others at the boat and traveled unimpeded to the meeting spot and were standing guard as GB Team Alpha unloaded their gear.

As soon as the others arrived Habib grabbed Jamaal and said, "We know he's in there. There is a meeting of the Azad leaders going on. Our timing is perfect."

Jamaal just smile.

Orin nodded to Jamaal and then pulled out the satellite photos again. It was time to cement the temporary plan and bring it to reality. All eyes were on Orin and on the now map he drew up right on the photo showing the complex. He had everything marked out and started doling out what he thought would work the best. The plan was open for discussion if anyone disagreed.

Orin pointed to a spot on the satellite photo map, Peter, work your way to this spot and cover Nitro who will be planting the explosives here, here, here, and here. That should drop the entire complex. Right Nitro?"

"Good thought Orin but no. Here and here will drop these walls and give us access to where they're suppose to be holding Tell and his men, but if were going to implode the place then there and there won't do it. I need to get to this spot, this spot, this spot and this spot for that."

"Okay. Can you cover all those spots from where you are Peter?"

"You plant those thing Nitro. I'll keep them bastards off of you."

"You know if I put an insurgent bomb here, Nitro pointed again, it will make a hell of a fire. That will keep a whole bunch of them rushing to put it out. It might distract enough of them so when I blow the wall we'll have less men to contend with."

Orin replied, "Great, but there's no way Pete can cover you from where he is. It's a good idea, but if you get caught, we're done."

"I can do it," said Jamaal. "They'll never see me I'll blend right in. Just tell me what to do Nitro."

"This could work," said Orin "I like it."

Nitro gave Jamaal specific instructions and pointed on the satellite map exactly where to plant the explosive firebomb.

"What about me Orin? What do you want me to do?"

"Joe if you can get here, you can cover Jamaal."

"Will, do."

Orin continued, "Nitro, does the firebomb have a timer on it?"

"No, I have remotes for all the charges."

"Great, then Jamaal, you plant the firebomb and come back right here. You, Ishmal, Kareem, and Mohamad will cover us from here. Habib, are you known by the Azad?"

"No."

"Then just wonder around and keep your eyes open. If you see anything that looks like we've been detected, hall ass back here and warn Jamaal. If everything goes as planned, here's how it should go down. Jamaal plants the firebomb; at the same time Nitro will plant the charges. Peter can cover Nitro from his perch, and Joe can cover Jamaal. Jamaal it's only one small package and Nitro showed you where to place it. That spot in the wall is out of sight of passer bys. You shouldn't have a problem. Once you all get back here, we'll be ready. Nitro will ignite the firebomb. The commotion will start. A few minutes later Nitro blows the wall. That's when Peter, Joe and I will rush the building at the fallen wall. We'll more than likely have to shoot our way in, but if the info is correct we'll find Tully and his men close to where we enter. We'll each carry an extra M-14, hand them to the prisoners, and our inside force is doubled. We get the hell out of there and when we get clear, Nitro pushes the button and good-by building and good-by Abu Musab Kalib. Anybody disagree or have anything to add?"

Nitro spoke up, "Orin, Jamaal should be the one to push the button. You don't need me here for that. I should go with you guys. One more gun can't hurt. Plus I'm pretty sure Jamaal here would like to be the one to implode this complex and bring the whole fucking thing down on Kalib and most of his army's heads and put an end to Kalib's rein."

"What do you say Jamaal?" asked Orin.

"Thank you Nitro my friend."

"Nitro answered, "You're welcome Jamaal, just one thing. Make sure all our asses our out of that fucking building before you push this button.

Everyone laughed.

Joe spoke up next and said, "Okay, let's say all this works and we have Tell and the other men. How the hell are we getting out of there?

Orin smiled and said, "We improvise."

"We improvise. The place will be swarming with Azad and we'll have some very weak prisoners with us and you're saying improvise," said Joe.

"Anybody got any ideas?" asked Orin.

Peter said, "I do. If the place is ablaze, I'll bet you dollars to donuts there will be plenty of ambulances around. We grab a couple of those and hightail it to the boat.

"Perfect, great idea," said Orin. "You know Peter you're not just a pretty face."

"I didn't think you noticed," replied Peter.

All the men laughed again.

They were sitting there getting ready to execute a mission that was nearly impossible, with every one of their lives in serious jeopardy, and they were laughing.

Right then they picked up there gear and got ready to bring their plan to life.

Peter was first. He had to get to his position without being seen. Not that easy when you're carrying a 7.62 MM sniper rifle, but so far luck was on GB Team Alpha's side. Peter was in position. At the same time Joe got to where he needed to get so he could cover Jamaal.

Next was Jamaal and Nitro turn, again, no problem. They all returned safely, mission accomplished.

The Americans and the Bakstana men were all set.

"Well, it's now or never," said Orin.

Nitro let loose the firebomb. BOOM, one side of the complex was a blaze. People were scrambling around like ants. Five minutes later GB Team Alpha was armed and ready. BOOM a much bigger explosion and the south end wall of the complex came tumbling down. Peter and crew were on the move. They were inside in less than a minute and the shooting started. They couldn't advance as quickly as they had wished, there were more Azad men shooting at them then they had hoped but every minute there were less. Two hand grenades later and Peter and Joe rushed the remaining guards. The Azad had no chance. Bodies were everywhere and luckily none of them were GB Team Alpha's. They quickly made their ways to the holding cells. Joe and Nitro were blowing locks of cells as they went freeing every prisoner they came across. Peter and Orin located Tully and his men; they were standing against the bars trying to see what was happening. Finally Tully saw Peter and Orin rounding the corner. The smile on John Tully's face was indescribable.

Tully looked up at Peter and Orin and said, "What took you so long?"

Peter answered, "Traffic."

They blew the cell door, armed Tully and his men and headed back the same way as they came. They met up with Joe and Nitro. There was no time to hug their compatriot, there was still work to be done, but Tully did get out a, "Hi guys!"

They all smiled, put their heads down and rushed the next corridor not knowing who would be standing there holding guns. Peter was ready to lead when Tully grabbed his shoulder and said, "Me first."

The weakened John Tully was not going to let any of his friends take a bullet that was meant for him.

Tully turned the corner. Rifle blazing. Two Azad were turning the opposite corner at the same time. The key word was, were. Tully gunned them down before they got a chance to raise their rifles. The open wall was near. The men slowed to see if the coast was clear. Four Azad soldiers stationed themselves on either side of the opening, just waiting for prisoners to try and escape. They thought they had it figured out. They were wrong. Bullets were flying from Jamaal and his men's vantage point. Four more Azad militia, dead.

Peter, Orin, Joe, and Nitro were the first to exit the complex through what use to be a wall. Tully and his men were close behind. They all made it safely back to the rendezvous spot.

"God damn, Joe, Nitro, Peter, Orin. It's good to see you," said Tully. "Who's your friends?"

"These guys saved your life. That's who they are. This man is Jamaal Geshal. He's the head of the Bakstana underground."

"I don't know how to thank you," said Tully.

"You will see. We will be thanking you as soon as Nitro gives me the signal."

Nitro nodded his head.

BOOM, BOOM, BOOM, BOOM, BOOM, BOOM, went the well-placed charges. Less than one minute later. There was no complex, just a giant cloud of dust and a big pile of concrete.

The Bakstana underground men did not verbally cheer as not to give their position away, but their arms were flying up in the air in victory.

Jamaal look at the carnage with a smile and said, "FUCK YOU Abu Musab Kalib."

GB Team Alpha along with Tully and his men just smiled.

Orin then said, "Let's get the hell out of here."

"Thank you my friends. I owe you my life," spouted Tully.

"Shut up," said Peter.

"Joe then said, "Don't thank us yet Tell. We still need to get out of here."

Just as Peter predicted, there were a number of ambulanced arriving every minute. The men broke up into two groups and commandeer two of the ambulances. Again the plan worked to perfection. As they sped away they were taking fire from the few Azad that were still left alive. They were peppered with bullets but again luck was on their side.

That's what they thought at first, and then Orin slumped over.

He was hit.

Conti III
Change is Coming

Chapter 34

Peter was at Orin's side in seconds.

"Orin, Orin," yelled Peter.

No response.

Blood was everywhere. It took a few valuable seconds to see where he was hit. He took a bullet in the back just above his clavicle bone and just below his left shoulder. Orin was lucky the bullet went clean through without hitting any bone or any organ, thank God. The other reason he was lucky. He was sitting in an ambulance equipped with everything Peter needed to stop the bleeding and get antiseptic bandages on both wounds, front and back.

Orin was only out a minute and snapped back to reality as Peter was administering first aid.

"How bad is it buddy?" asked Orin.

"You'll live. The bullet went clean through. You lost a lot of blood, but I got it stopped."

With that Peter had an IV in Orin before he knew it.

Orin asked, "Anybody else hit."

"No Pal, you won that honor."

Orin laughed a painful laugh. "If you have to leave me, leave me. You hear."

Peter just laughed and said to Joe who was driving, "Orin is trying to be a hero. It's hilarious."

Joe responded, "How is he Peter?"

"He got hit in the shoulder and the bullet went clean through. He'll be alright, but we're definitely down a man."

"Glad to hear that. As far as where we are, we haven't lost distance between us and the other ambulance, we're still right behind Nitro," answered Joe.

"Do we have anyone following us?" asked Peter.

"Not yet, but you can bet your ass we will," answered Joe.

Jamaal, in Nitro's ambulance, was providing directions to Nitro and Joe was following right behind.

They somehow made it to where the boat was tethered without being detected. Nitro, Tully and Jamaal were shocked and upset when Peter got out of the ambulance with Orin draped all over him.

"Jesus Christ is he alright?" yelled Nitro.

"He was hit back there when they were shooting at the ambulances, but he's going to be okay. He was hit in the shoulder and the bullet went through."

"Thank God," said Tully.

"Give me a hand with him. Let's get him in the boat and lay him down before he starts to bleed again."

They loaded everyone in the boat along with most of the weapon they still had and were off. They hoped the Azad wouldn't know they came in by water, but that was a long shot. They had to figure that they did. You could bet the river patrols were informed and looking for them.

They were going as fast as the fishing boat could move and hadn't come across any of the enemy. Then they came around a bend in the river and there they were, three Azad patrol boats waiting for them. The second they were seen, the enemy started shooting at them. Ishmal turned the boat around immediately and the patrol boats were in pursuit. Peter and Joe grabbed the handheld 50 cals and were returning fire as fast as they were receiving it. The lead patrol boat took a shell obviously to the gas tank because it blew up like a fireworks display on the fourth of July. The other two boats where gaining. Nitro and Tully jumped next to Joe and Peter and started shooting as well. Jamaal was right behind them. All of a sudden Peter disappeared, when he reemerged, he was holding a missile launcher.

Whoosh, a missile was fired. A few seconds later, there was only one patrol boat chasing them. Joe grabbed the other missile launcher, ran to the front of the boat and yelled to Ishmal to make a u-turn and head straight for the chasing patrol boat. Ishmal did just that and as soon as they were face to face, Joe fired. Whoosh, then there were none.

As they continued towards Telerude their boat passed a number of Azad men that were floating in the water after being thrown from their patrol boats. They were still alive, but not for long. As they passed them Kareem and Mohamad finished the job, killing their enemy by letting loose machine gun fire at the swimming Azad malitia. They showed no mercy, just like the Azad showed them for the last six months.

Peter immediately checked on Orin. He was passed out. He must have lost more blood than they thought.

"Get this fucking boat going faster. Orin's in trouble," yelled Peter.

The three patrol boats must have been their entire compliment in that section because the battered crew of the fishing boat did not have to face any more of them. They made it to the hidden combat jeeps safe and sound without anyone else being injured or worse killed. They got Orin in one of the jeeps and as comfortable as they could, but this was going to be a rough ride. All the guys were worried. Not that they might be fighting more Azad, but for Orin.

They took off and were not shy about moving at a rapid pace. If they ran into more Azad they would just have to battle them.

They did.

Not ten miles from the boarded an Azad ambush was set up. Had to be twenty men. As the three combat jeeps came over a hill there they were.

Peter, in the lead jeep, with Nitro driving yelled to Nitro, "Fuck it, lets attack the bastards."

With that Peter manned his fifty Cal machine gun and started firing. Joe followed Peter's lead and grabbed his jeeps turret, and Tully stepped infront of Jamaal to grab his jeeps.

"I got this Jamaal," yelled Tully.

The three Green Beret teammates let the Azad have it like they had never seen before. They had killed three quarters of them before the others ran. Not a single man on the jeeps was harmed. The three jeeps raced to the boarder.

Just before they were across, another small ambush was set up. The Azad weren't about to let these people back into Saudi. This time the jeeps spotted them in time and squealed to a halt.

"What do you want to do Peter?" asked Joe.

The question was answered for them.

The Azad ambushers were slaughter from behind by Colonel Ashan and his men who were there just in case something like this was to take place.

The jeeps rolled into Saudi Arabia territory and stopped next to Colonel Ashan's vehicle.

The Colonel got out of his truck and walked over to the men exiting their jeeps.

"Unbelievable," he said.

"Thanks for the assist Colonel," said Peter.

"I wasn't about to let you guys do everything by yourselves. Screw the orders. Congratulations men. Unbelievable. Simply unbelievable." The Colonel turned to the prisoners and said, "Major Tully I presume."

"It sure is nice to see you Colonel. Thanks for your help."

"We did nothing Major. These brave men you rode in with did it all."

Tully just nodded his head in agreement and said, "They sure are something. Have been since I met them and these Bakstana men are some brave people. My thanks go out to them. As far as my team and friends. I have no words."

Jamaal walked over to the Colonel and said, "These Americans won us back our country. Kalib and his Generals are dead. Bakstana is free. I have never seen braver men and I don't think I ever will. Thank your president from all the Bakstana people for sending such men here."

GB Alpha team saluted the Bakstana men and then they all hugged.

With that going down Major Olsen was being lifted from his place in the jeep.

"Oh no. Is he alright?" said a concerned Colonel.

Peter answered in his lighthearted way even though he was scared to death for Orin, "The normal man wouldn't make it, but Major Orin Olsen, he's not normal.

"Let's get this man to the infirmary back at the base. NOW!" yelled the Colonel to some of his men. "And GB Team Alpha, I need to be debriefed. Not only for militarily reasons but I just want to know how you did this. This is unbelievable. Let's move out."

Jamaal and his men were getting ready to head out. The GB Team were saying their good-bys and as they did Peter pulled Jamaal over to the side and said, "Jamaal, load up one of these jeeps with these weapons and take them with you. If anyone asks where the shit is, I'll say we had to leave stuff behind in one of the battles. Thank you my friend, you are one brave man."

"That is funny coming from you and your team. I, and all of the Bakstana people thank you Peter Conti and all of GB Team Alpha. You will never be forgotten."

With that said, he was gone.

Back at Riyadh while Orin was being attended to, the team debriefed Colonel Ashan. The Colonel listened intently and wrote down all that was said. He didn't say this, but he needed this information exactly how it occurred. Big time medals were going to be given for this. Maybe even the Congressional.

As soon as they were finished Peter was looking for a phone.

"Mrs. Conti," said Peter.

"OH my God. Oh my God. Thank you God. Peter are you alright?"

"I'm fine honey and so is Tully."

Jenny was crying.

"Jenny, everything is fine. Only."

"Oh no. Only what?"

"Orin was hit."

"Is he?" she asked.

"No, he's too ornery for that, but he'll be laid up for a bit."

"Was anyone else injured?"

"Only the enemy sweetheart. Only the enemy."

THAT'S HOW IT HAPPENED. THAT'S HOW PETER CONTI CHANGED FROM THE HEAD OF A MAFIA FAMILY TO ONE OF THE MOST HONERED MEN IN OUR COUNTRY. WHERE HE GOES FROM HERE, WHO KNOWS? WHAT ABOUT GB TEAM ALPHA, WILL THEY BE CALLED UPON AGAIN, ANOTHER WHO KNOWS?

RIGHT NOW ALL PETER CONTI WANTS IS TO GO BACK HOME TO THE AWAITING ARMS OF THE WOMAN HE LOVES.

THE END

Made in the USA
Monee, IL
29 July 2020